# FEMERON

Michael Alan Shapiro

FEMERON
Copyright © 1978, 2020 Michael Alan Shapiro

ISBN: 978-7356389-3-5

All rights reserved. No part of this publication may be reproduced, stored in a retrieval system, or transmitted in any form or by any means, electronic, mechanical, recording or otherwise, without the prior written permission of the author.

Published by
Stone Street Publishing
Orlando, Florida.

Publisher's Note: This is a work of fiction; names, characters, places, and incidents are a product of the author's imagination. Locales and public names are sometimes used for atmospheric purposes. Any resemblance to actual people, living or dead, or to businesses, companies, events, institutions, or locales is completely coincidental.


Printed on acid-free paper.

Stone Street Publishing 2020


Contact the Author:
On Facebook Page: Femeron

Other Novels by

Michael Alan Shapiro

*On Thunder Road*

*Inner Lights*

*Raman Shah*

*The Cross of Chorrillos*

# Forward
## By Noelle Petersen

Cars propelled by magnetic power, computer screens and watches projecting hologram images of movie stars into the room for you to dance with, laser guns with devastating fire power, the ubiquitous Star Trek inspired Laser Particle Transport system and the highly imaginative female dominated society and government; all conceived and used to perfection by Michael Shapiro in his science fiction masterwork, Femeron.

Beyond the entertainment factor however, there are very serious issues Mr. Shapiro is presenting. Though he clothes the story in an amusing and satirical style, one that takes the Battle of the Sexes to new heights, he shows us that even as the world strives to clean up its act; even as the self- proclaimed enlightened ones strive to save the planet from the effects of over-population, still in reality there are more than seven and a half billion of us. Our daily activities multiplied by seven billion contribute each day to pollution and the deforestation of the planet and to the resultant habitat loss that foretells the extinction of not only other animal species but of the human species as well.

The seriousness of his predictions and the ironic twist that the very people who have developed medical treatments and medicines to reduce mortality rates along with the people who in all good consciousness are working against abortion funding.

These same people who are adamant to the point of hysteria about saving the planet are in actuality contributing to and invigorating the overpopulation problem.

Shapiro points out, individuals who do not consider the resources needed by each of their offspring, due to ignorance one assumes, bring forth new pressures on the ecosystem with each birth. That the more prosperous individuals and countries are inspired to provide food and medicine for those children while well intentioned, do they not actually guarantee the destruction of the planet that they so honestly want to save?

In the novel, the super-rich families on earth are using cloning methods of promulgation to ensure the survival of their genes and bloodlines while ignoring the plight of the poor and homeless outside of the Femeron borders. Have these people become selfish to the point of being sociopaths? Was there ever a time when humans were not selfish? Does his hypothesis mean that for the good of the planet we should forsake our fellow beings?

What are the ethical and moral obligations that we each have to our fellow human beings and their children?

Life on earth is threatened. Will no one deal with these issues even as so many see the writing on the wall? Our super success as a species has ignited the candle that has shed light on the truths revealed in nature but our species' success has also lit the stick of dynamite, a manmade substance that will ultimately destroy us. Have we gone past the tipping point?

Is there any hope, any plan or method to adopt that will change the inevitable? The earth shall cleanse itself, one of the characters in the novel tells us. Meaning the planet will rid itself of a species that over-populates and dominates to the point of self-destruction. Is that our destiny?

"We should put our best people on it," another of the characters suggests and one has to agree that this above all other issues needs to be addressed by a diversity of well educated, serious individuals, male and female, black and white, progressive and conservative.

# Chapter One
## Time has Come Today

Year: 2090

The buildings in the downtown Femeron capital city are tall and angular with stores and shops on the street level and apartments on the floors above. The apartment of Lolan 11 is in one of the new buildings. Her furniture and appliances are chrome and glass. Everything sparkles under bright lighting. Lolan is dressed in a casual jumpsuit as she prepares a meal in the kitchen. She considers a list of photos that hang mid-air in 3-D hologram images. She selects one and in moments it appears behind one of the cubby holes in a white cabinet. Taking the small meal, she sits at the breakfast bar between the kitchen and the living room. A computer in the living room sounds a quiet, "dong" and a blue light comes on above the large telescreen.

"Go," she says with a mouthful.

The computer, now free to communicate with her does so in a low, smooth female voice.

"Lolan Eleven?"

"The same," she answers as she flips a page of a hologram magazine on the breakfast bar counter.

"You have placed your number in the milking pool drawing, have you not?"

Lolan, in the middle of taking another bite stops and looks at the screen. "What are you taking a survey? To the point or shut down."

"The numbers are in and yours was among those chosen."

"Cool," Lolan nods as she takes another bite. "You will depart central at one tenth north star and..."

"Which playgroup," Lolan interrupts.

"Male Group 47. Inner city, section 39, cross section 9th and..."

"Alright, alright. I know where it is." Then to herself, "Group 47, hmm, they have some nice asses in that group." She takes a moment to chew her food and then to the computer, "Tele, show me a list of playas in that group."

Rows of photos of the different males in playgroup 47 appears on the large telescreen. One at a time each photo is blown up. First a head shot, then photos of their body. Underneath each photo is their description with their height, weight and physical dimensions. Each has a short description of their interests.

"Okay, Tele, shut down," Lolan orders after having made a mental note of who she is interested in.

The screen goes black, the blue light turns off. Lolan takes the final bite of her meal and goes over to the couch in the living room. She opens a console on the glass coffee table and the image of a small keyboard comes up. She types in her instructions with both thumbs, fast and accurate. When she completes her input, the telescreen comes back on and music begins to play a Latin tune with a dance beat. As the music plays, three dimensional images come off the screen and float into the room. They are life-size, hologram images of two movie stars; a male who looks and carries himself like a young Elvis and a female star from the latest popular film. The images dance around the living room and Lolan gets up and dances with them. When she leans in, the images lean back. She laughs in gleeful pleasure at being able to interact with famous movie stars. For their part, the images are laughing, dancing and flirting with Lolan. Elvis, in light purple slacks and a white, short sleeve shirt with his collar up, comes close to Lolan. He starts to grind and Lolan laughs again. The female image, dressed in a dark pink, skin tight plastic one piece, laughs and also grinds on her.

After the song ends a new beat begins but Lolan is interrupted by a "dong" and a blue light on the screen. She stops dancing and calls out, "wait". The images stop dancing but they continue to move about, watching her to see when she'll be ready to renew their dance.

"What is it Tele?"

"Incoming message from Dr. Joy," the teleprompter's female voice announces.

"Okay, go," Lolan says and a new image, this of a woman in her early forties floats out from the screen. She has blonde shoulder length hair and is wearing the white jump suit and coat of a medical researcher. The figure stands in front of Lolan and smiles.

"Lolan, how are you?"

"I'm fine, and you doctor?"

"I apologize for disturbing your personal time but I needed to send you this message. I have urgent business that I would like your help with."

"Certainly, of course," Lolan sits on the couch and the image of Dr. Joy stands in front of her.

"We have an important meeting in three days at the Femeron Genetics Advisory Board." "Yes, I'm aware of that," Lolan nods.

The Elvis hologram has come across the room and is flirting with the image of Dr. Joy. She laughs when he begins to dance next to her; doing the shimmy with both arms outstretched to his sides. Dr. Joy's image looks embarrassed and interested at the same time. Lolan laughs along with her.

"Okay, well off you go then," Lolan says and with a short wave of her arm, both of the other two images evaporate.

"He's cute," Dr. Joy straightens her uniform.

"Yes, extremely. Great dancer too," Lolan agrees.

"Well, anyway, to the point," Dr. Joy's image continues. "I would like you to prepare a background synopsis of all participants. I want to know going in where they each stand on issues of male captivity. Have they ever made public or private statements? What do their school records show? That sort of thing and yes of course their political stance."

"You do recall that I have been working on that project for two weeks?" Lolan asks.

"Yes, I know, but I need to add two additional research scientists whose attendance has just been announced."

"I see," Lolan nods. "Okay, well send that information to my station and I will work on it."

"Lolan, I need that entire project by tomorrow evening so I have the time to study it."

"By tomorrow evening? Hmm, well." Lolan takes a moment to calculate the steps required. She nods, "Okay, yes. I can finish it up by then." Lolan gets up from the couch. "Is there anything else?"

"No," Dr. Joy says. "Thank you for your time." The image bows her head, palms together in front of her. "Stay well and contact me as soon as you can."

"I will, Doctor," Lolan waves her arm and the image of Dr. Joy evaporates.

Lolan puts the music back on and still dancing, she goes into her bedroom off the living room. Her mattress floats in the middle of the bedroom and she sits on the edge of it and rubs the leg of someone under the paper-thin covers. Lolan shakes the body awake by nudging it again.

"Hey, Cee-na? Cee-anne? Come on. Wake up. I've news."

"Huh?" A groggy female voice sounds from underneath.

"My number's come up at central. I'm going milking tonight."

"Mmm, sounds nice. Which playgroup?" Cee-na sits up and smiles at Lolan.

"Number forty-seven."

"Forty-seven? Okay, wait. Let me think. Yes, I've been there. Try to find...I think his name is Jay-15. He is sooo funny and a fine piece too."

"I know him," Lolan says "and you're right, he is a nut. There are a lot of crazies in that group come to think of it. It should be a ball, right?"

"Absolutely," Cee-na says as she gets up and crosses the room and begins to dress. Unlike Lolan 11 who was cloned with particular attention paid to her physical attributes; she is tall and fit, with high cheek bones and perfect breasts, Cee-na is square in body and plain of face. And where Lolan has on a well fitted, tailored jumpsuit, Cee-na quickly dresses in several bright, multi- colored skirts and blouses. With her layered look to her liking, she messes up her tri-colored hair with both hands, fixing her short hair so as to look just as rumbled as her dresses.

She walks back to Lolan and kisses her on the mouth. "Have fun tonight, darlin'. I've got to get to class." As she goes out the bedroom door she adds over her shoulder, "I'll call you in a few days."

Cee-na walks through the living room, passing large picture windows through which she sees a panoramic view of tall skyscrapers. At the far end of the room, she touches a panel and a two-meter section of the wall slides open revealing a small room. Cee-na inputs instructions onto a control panel and when she has completed her programing, the computer responds with a quiet 'ding-dong' and above the door, blue and green lights spell out, 'Laser Particle Transport System, All Clear'. Bands of laser lights hum across the door's opening. The lights vibrate high energy but Cee-na, without any concern, steps into the light and disappears.

\*\*\*

## CLASS ROOM: CENTRAL DISTRICT

Lively space music plays as female students enter an amphitheater classroom. As the young students find their seats, the room darkens and sharp, quick flashes of colored laser lights shoot across the high ceilings. The lights rip through the air, their effect much like a firework's display over the students' heads. The young women scream and shout as the display reaches a crescendo. When almost all are in their seats, the music's volume drops down and the light show ceases. Telescreens turn on in front of each student's console as the classroom quiets. The video playing on their screens is of a downtown metropolitan city in the first decades of the twenty-first century. Cee-na enters the front of the classroom and walks over to the speaker's podium.

"Today's discussion," she says as she looks around the packed classroom, "is an historical summary of our Femeron society. Your assignment was to prepare an analysis of how we came out of the male dominated cultures of the past." She continues without taking a breath.

"She like has a tendency to run her sentences together, doesn't she? A student in the front of the classroom asks her friend.

"And her voice is soo whiny," the other student agrees.

"Wait until she warms to the subject matter, she'll go totally hysterical on us," the first student says and they both laugh.

The telescreens show different cosmopolitan cities at rush hour and close ups of pedestrians' faces. "These scenes are examples of the population in the early twenty-first century," Cee-na says.

The videos of the pedestrians fighting their way through traffic appear on the small desk screens as well as on the large screen behind Cee-na. The pedestrians are in a frenzied hurry. They bump each other thoughtlessly and jostle their way through the crowded sidewalks. In the street, cars are honking their horns at each other.

"Life in this masculine created society is a living hell for its citizens. They suffer a thousand varieties of neurosis and phobias. Incredible you think. Yes, well *incredible* it was! Human beings leading unhappy, lonely lives. It saddens us even now to look back at the way it was for them. The more we study their case histories, the more we understand the devastating effect masculine societies had on individuals.

"Aprilla," Cee-na points to a student with her hand up. "Can you share with us what your feelings and observations were when you read about these past times?"

"Pathetic," Aprilla says. "This monstrous way of life produced the ultimate pathos for people. Why are some families rich while others can't afford even a vacation home?"

"That is not the worst part, Aprilla," another student speaks up. "Why is there so much violence?" she asks.

"Yes, violence," Cee-na nods her head. "You see, for that reason, we must study the past. The lessons learned from studying masculine created and dominated cultures are crucial. Indeed, the emergence of our own, Femeron society, was born in logical reaction to this madness."

Cee-na stops and lets the video scenes tell the story. The students watch videos from world history; infamous moments of marching armies, civil rights disturbances and the clubbing to death of baby seals.

"Why all the violence?" Cee-na asks. "How did society develop into this hell?"

"Their leaders were all males," a student in the back of the classroom calls out. "But what makes them so violent?

"And...and..well crazy?" another student asks.

"Yes, why?" Cee-na asks. "Well the answer to that question came in the late nineteen nineties when scientific breakthroughs in the field of genetics proved that the Y genes of the male species were in fact *incomplete* X genes."

On the telescreens, a large blue Y symbol is next to a blue X. As Cee-na explains the theory of the incomplete Y gene, a blue dotted line transforms the Y into an X by adding a leg on the right side.

"Males is other words, are incomplete females."

The room explodes in cheers and jeers. Cee-na holds up her hand to restore order.

"You think I'm exaggerating?" she says. "You know, female genes are double X, right? All of our genes are complete and whole while some of the genes in males are partial. They are incomplete and it shouldn't surprise anyone that a deficient gene will have an effect on how that person develops. We know from our studies that males in fact do develop differently due to their gene deficiency."

"I'm lost," a young female calls out. "How does this discovery relate back to the sorry state of the human race?"

Students' hands shoot up around the classroom.

Cee-na points to a student and calls her name, "ShaRona."

"Turns out that the male's incomplete genetic chemistry has had two major effects on their development," ShaRona stands as she addresses her classmates. "The first effect was to cause them to not fully develop either emotionally or psychologically. We've read studies that showed how this is reflected in their personalities. Their entire sex is a perfect example of egocentric mania."

"Give us an example, ShaRona," Cee-na asks.

"Well, this is demonstrated over and over by the male's total lack of empathy towards other living beings."

"Very good, ShaRona," Cee-na says. "You're quite right. The male's superego is clearly seen in their inability to empathize with other life forms. They don't even have empathy for their own species!" Cee-na bangs her fists on the podium which draws cheers from some of the students. "These sociopathic characteristics, they are the base on which man's economic and social institutions were built. Ev*erything* in fact that males created, were all created solely to satisfy *their* physical and emotional needs and no one else's!"

"But if they are so…so..crude, how did they get all the power?" Aprilla re-enters the discussion.

"Evolution needed their increased size and strength to protect and provide for their young." Cee-na explains. "It was that survival strategy that enabled the human species to succeed."

"Yes, but we don't need them for survival anymore, do we?" A student near Aprilla asks.

"It is difficult to understand," Cee-na nods her head in agreement. "How did males continue their reign over the human race, even when there was no need for them?"

"But wasn't there a need for them?" ShaRona asks. "I mean, they built things. They are energetic and work hard to create things. Things that females were unable to build like building and bridges."

"Yes, all true," Cee-na agrees. "Until of course robots and advanced mechanics allowed females to build without the need for brute strength. But let's not forget their other great talent," Cee-na says. "They held unto their positions of power by violence or threats of violence, sure but also because they developed an amazing talent for *Salesmanship*!"

The students shout cheers and jeers to her remark.

Cee-na holds both her palms facing forward and bows her head as if dispelling any protest or argument from among her audience. She looks up and says, "The masculine ability to make even the most insane deviltries appear logical, meaningful and *necessary* for one's survival is true genius. They are masters in being able to convince other intelligent beings of anything that they want them to believe. True geniuses." She nods her head in confident, affirmative agreement with the cheers and boos of her students.

Cee-na walks around the podium. "Exactly how so *many* people were so *blind* to these masculine myths? And how *so* many were kept from using their own *reasoning* minds still remains a mystery to this day. And what is the most amazing example of this salesmanship? I refer you to the one, the only, The Money-Work System!"

Applauds and cheering interrupt her.

"Rudimentary at first," she continues but has to shout over the students' ruckus. "The money-work system developed into the most complex, powerful force in the masculine created society." The classroom grows quiet and she continues. "From seashells to gold, from silver and diamonds to pieces of paper; the myth of 'value' and 'worth' prospered while the lives of the tribal members became exceedingly cheap.

"With money there is power and as long as everyone played the game and they all did, male and female alike, the males would retain their power. Despite the fact that everyone suffered except the very few who mastered the system. For example, look at how the earth's resources were controlled by a handful of males. Those resources, oil, diamonds, iron ore for example, they all rightly belong to all of humankind, but they were pulled from the earth and sold like they were created only for those few families. People under this economic villainy stopped relating to each other. They lost their compassion, became mired in the game of money as they wallowed in the money-work system!"

Cee-na pauses, allows the energy to come down. In a lower voice and more somber she continues. "Slowly, very, slowly, it became obvious to the people that they were being led through life by an unfit group. Only after many catastrophes and crisis, did the thought occur to them that it did not have to be the way it was. And ever so slowly did it begin to change. Yet the struggle was not centered, or organized. As one of our Founding Mothers, Mazie Hirono, said at the time; "All men need to Shut Up!!"

The video of the American Congresswoman from Hawaii plays on the screen. Standing in the capital building, she shouts her epitaph and the young students erupt in loud cheers. Cee-na allows the commotion to die down.

"The solution," she continues, "came from the field of genetics, where two important discoveries occurred. First, as we have seen, we learned that the male's Y gene was a deficient X gene. From this discovery, a theory developed which stated that man's evolutionary energies were blocked by this incomplete Y gene. The energy not used there had flowed instead to other areas of his development, his physical branches. Yes, he was bigger and stronger than females. Yes, he could run faster and leap higher but his more subtle development, his emotional and psychological development, those areas were stunted.

"In correlation with this theory of the males' faulty evolution, there developed a proof that females were more balanced. That we were fully development. Fully evolved. This theory, called the Femeron Theory of Evolution, and its proof brought the realization that cultural systems created by males were the products of a deficient source. The Femeron Theory explained that the masculine ego was the sour fruit born of the male's deficient cellular chemistry. Why then should intelligent beings allow their lives and their happiness, the well-being of planet in fact, be in the hands of less evolved creatures? Would intelligent people allow themselves to be ruled by chimps and gorillas? Of course not! Societies should be ruled by a higher, more evolved beings, WOMEN!!"

Applause, cheers and whistles.

"One must realize though that even the brightest of males could not grasp the truths of these proven genetic theories. Socrates, Lennon, Marx, Kennedy, Che; all men have always envisioned a world in which males are to be in the position of authority. Such outrageous self-conceit, don't you think?"

More applause and whistles from around the room.

"Their blindness never allowed them to glimpse the truth about themselves and their sex as a whole. Not even after these irrefutable truths were known, could they understand and accept their deficiencies. They fought to dispel these ugly rumors. Their scientists stifled the teaching of the Femeron Theory. Meanwhile another breakthrough in the field of genetics occurred. This second breakthrough was the tool awaiting its time of need. I am referring to the refinement of a proficient method of cloning. When we could reproduce a human offspring without the need to use the male sperm, without the need to introduce their deficient male Y gene into the equation. A new race of females could be promulgated. This method of improved cloning techniques stood ready for use as the breeding system of an enlightened civilization."

"That's all well and good," a young student calls out from the corner of the classroom, "that cloning stuff and the X and Y gene stuff, but what about the threat of nuclear war? I read that it was the threat of nuclear war that led the world to dismantle the male governments."

"This is true, Benita," Cee-na nods her head. "Very true, as you read, events took place which brought about this radical but necessary replacement of the male dominated societies. In the middle of the twenty-first century those events brought enlightenment to billions of individuals almost simultaneously. The combined strength of these billions of concerned humans could not be bought off. The powers that be could not convince the populace to kill each other for the sake of Country, God or Money. No, this time the people rose up as one because they could see and they understood what was at stake."

Cee-na pauses to take a sip of water.

"The dam of ignorance is not easily broken," she continues. "Only one reality has the power to produce *instant* revelation and that is the sight of death. Not the news reports of someone else's death but the clear, unmistakable sight of your own death as it approaches you, not later but *right now*!

"This close sighting of the Dark Angel came to the world's population in the mid twenty-first century as a nuclear holocaust was only days away. The world watched as the super powers clashed. The peoples' hope for a dialogue that would diminish the danger became less likely with each insult. With each new provocation the world populace held their collective breaths. Everyone understood that this impending holocaust would be the end of human life. Even to the women and children of Arabia, Iran, China, India, Russia, The United States and to the ends of the earth; everyone knew the irreversible end of all human life on earth was about to happen. The world's population knew that many thousands of hydrogen bombs were armed and ready for launch. They knew that in response to the first strike, there would be multiple counterstrikes. Counterstrikes answered by more counterstrikes, repeated launches, until the entire worldwide arsenal was spent. This meant that thousands of thermonuclear weapons would all be detonated within hours of each other. From such an event, only the truly unfortunate would survive, and survive only to live in hell on earth for a short time."

Cee-na reaches down and enters instructions into the master computer so that a poem from that terrifying time comes up on the students' screens.

"This was written by a lowly seamstress in Turkey during the crisis. She posted this on the internet." Cee-na reads out loud as her students follow the poem on their viewing consoles.

"'The *whole* planet's gonna blow apart and become an asteroid belt traveling in pieces 'round the sun. Worse than this, your children ain't gonna have *no* children, so don't worry 'bout the rent, Sista! Just listen to those bastards rant and yell but it's *OUR* lives they gonna send to hell."

Cee-na is interrupted by applause for this unknown poetess.

"As you can see, this doom realization was a real flash of lightening across the cerebral movie screen called the mind. This produced in individuals across the globe a resolute character. A character strong and devoted to the belief in a world sisterhood. A sisterhood they called Mistersogynists. That is Mister-sah-gee- nists, haters of men. It was a sisterhood led by our founding mothers, Greta Thornberg and Mozie Hirono, both of whom despised everything male."

The screens show a video of an interview with Greta Thonberg. Her left eye is twitching with seething rage as she pounds the table and yells,
"How DARE you!"

"It was a sisterhood of females that would no longer put up with masculine cultures." Cee-na nods her head to emphasize the righteousness of their cause. "A Sisterhood of *billions* of women, young and old who saw with disgust how masculine governed societies turned the God-like consciousness of an infant into hate filled, killing adults. These humanitarian feelings are what created the critical surge of female power. It was a female revolution that pushed its way through from the inner feelings of individuals to the very heights of governance. Their sorrows and rage gave birth to a world-wide movement that demanded that this madness must end.

"Even males finally realized this truth and they along with females, began to look at all aspects of their male dominated cultures in a new light. They saw that this myth of male superiority was too dangerous a belief for it to be allowed to continue. Genetic scientists were ready then with the tools to implement the answer; cloning. And with cloning the ultimate end to masculine control."

Cee-na pauses to take a question from one of the young female students, "Why then are there *any* males left today? I mean, if they are of no use?"

"They're a menace!" another student interjects.

"Totally!" a third student shouts out.

"Males are kept alive and are regenerated in limited numbers for two reasons," Cee-na says. "First of all, they are used as playthings and do in fact provide us with some diversion. Secondly, because as you know from your biology and world food source classes that we are running out of the ability to provide food for the entire world population and since male sperm is pure protein, males are used to provide us with their semen. It's a delicacy and also an important food source for millions of our peoples. Male semen, milked from the captive male population and placed into a special growth culture, multiples rapidly. The result is an abundant supply of protein supplement."

"Isn't it also true," a young black girl asks, "that because cloning evolves and may be less effective or begin to produce mutants, that it may be important at some point to reintroduce male sperm back into the process of re-creation?"

"Yes, there are some scientists who argue that we must have available the natural ingredients for procreation." Cee-na agrees. "That's true and yes, certainly they believe that we must always have some males in the population. That was a major reason."

Cee-na appears to half agree with that logic but her voice is not as forceful as it had been.

# Chapter Two
## Life in a Playgroup

Seated in a circle around a video screen, six men are using their hand-held devices to play a game. Images and sounds from the screen's round, basketball size game board come flying out at the men who intercept the images with laser shots. The hologram images are ghosts of past warriors or small monsters that come into the room and grow very big very fast unless the men are able to "kill" them with a shot from their laser guns. If they fail, the monsters and warriors move about the room bothering everyone with their screams and insulting comments. The men's shouts and the game's sounds are the loudest noises in the room.

Other males, all dressed in silver colored jumpsuits, sit at tables reading or writing. Some are painting at easels. There are pairs of men playing electronic backgammon and chess. They each have belts around their waists with matching sneaker colors. There are black belts with black foot wear, green belts with green footwear, red, blue and a very few with white belts. The scene in the play room is shown on a large screen in another room where two females sit in front of the console. The guards wear matching tan, khaki uniform pant suits.

"Oh, Jo-ella, that H27 thinks he's so clever," one guard says as she watches the men. "He revels in those stupid games."

"Yeah, what a blinker!"* The second guard responds.

"Why can't these males see themselves for what they are?"

A section of the wall whooshes open behind them and the guards turn to greet six females. In the group is Lolan11. The six visitors are loose and laughing.

"Have you all come to party?" The guard, Joella asks.

"We're the Milking Party! Wooo-Woooo!" They celebrate and laugh as they walk up to the viewing screen and check out the males.

"Typical for them," the first guard points at the screen. "They're trying to outpoint each other to prove their prowess."

"It's incredible," Lolan11 says. "They compete at everything! I've even seen them make a game out of taking a piss!"

The other ladies laugh.

"No, it's true. They were measuring who could pee the furthest!"

They all laugh again.

"What fools!" another of the female visitors says.

"It's their genes" the guard, Jo-ella says. "They get penises instead of brains."

More laughter as the women continue to observe the males' activities.

In a few moments, one of the guards gets up from the console and exits the guard room with the visitors following behind her. Inside the play room, a section of a wall whooshes open and the six milkers and the one guard enter.

The men are surprised and very happy to see females. They all cheer and leave what they are doing to walk over to them. One male wolf-whistles, others shout out greetings.

"Oh, *baby*, you're looking good!" "Come here, honey, I'll treat you right."

"You're beautiful, you know that, right, baby?"

Another male is standing off to the side, reciting poetry.

His friend looks at him in amazement.

"What the hell are you doing?" he asks.

"I'm reading Sonnets by Shakespeare," the male responds. "I mean, what the hell. I've tried everything else. I'm going to show them my artistic side. See if that works."

"Right," the other nods his head. "Sounds like a plan."

The females are in a party mood. In their cool, confident way they are loose and free. They laugh as the men compete for their attention. Music comes on and the males use the thumping rhythm to show off their dance moves. The ladies join in and the entire room is full of gyrating dancers bouncing to the heavy beat. Images of famous movie stars and rock musicians float out from the wall screens and project out into the room. The hologram images move about and are dancing with the men and females. Fabio is dancing with Selma Hayek.

One female visitor holds her arms out to her sides, shakes her hair loose while she shimmies and shouts out to the men watching her.

"What do you like? Huh?"

The males hoot and holler. At the end of the song, the females intersperse among the males. They are picking and choosing in a carefree manner. For their part, the males are clowning and showing off.

Groups begin to leave the playroom and walk out into a long corridor. Off to each side of the corridor there are separate rooms and inside one room Lolan11 and another female milker have taken two males from the day room. They are sitting on a small couch.

"This is Serena, I'm Lolan," Lolan11 introduces herself. She stands and opens a cabinet drawer and takes out an apparatus. One of the males is feeling up Serena.

"Look," he says to her, "Check me out. I'm big and strong. Don't you think? You like strong bodies, don't you? Well I can lift 4000 klackos** Over my head!"

"Yes, you are both terrific," Serena says. "But you are getting too excited. When was the last time you were milked?"

"Relax now," Lolan says as she comes back to the couch and sits between the males. They both start to feel her up and she laughs and makes out with them.

Serena sets up the milking apparatus which is a short rubber hose with a glass test tube on the end of it. "Okay, we're good to go," she says. She takes the first male by the wrist and leads him over to a massage table.

"I'm set too," he says as he feels them both up.

They stroke him and he starts humping the air.

The females for their part are laughing but also getting hot, they take turns kissing the male and stroking him.

"I'm beautiful, right?' he asks "Don't you think?"

"And tough too," Serena says.

"Yes, I am," he says. "I can beat all of those other blinkers. I'm a *black belt*. See?" He points to his belt and shoes.

"Oh, yes you are. A Black Belt, wow." Lolan says sarcastically while smiling at Serena.

Things are really heating up now. All of his clothes are off. The two females hook him up to the tube and stroke him with hands and mouths.

"C'mon now, Black Belt," Lolan says. "We're on a mission here."

"All this work," Serena says, "oh if it wasn't so vital to our Femeron society, I don't know how I could put up with it." She's being sarcastic while, non-stop, he humps on her and feels her up.

"Oooh," Serena moans. She says this as her mouth pouts and she licks her lips with her sensuous tongue. She then bends down and starts to lick his member. Her hands play with her two companions. All of them are moving in rhythm. Each of them is getting hotter and more vehement in their love making. They moan and groan. Finally, the male climaxes in uncontrollable, blissful waves. His sperm fills the glass container.

"We've got enough to feed a friggin city!" Lolan says. "Way to shoot, man."

Serena laughs, a full belly laugh. She has to bend at her waist from the force of her laughter. Meanwhile, the male is collapsing. He is holding onto both females and they struggle to lift his weight off of them and guide him back to the couch. He is limp and weak. They laugh at him and take the wrists of the other male and pull him up off the couch and begin to stroke him.

---

*A blinker is a person who cannot see the psychological reasons for their own behavior. This type of person doesn't look into the eye of anyone who confronts them but blinks and looks elsewhere.

** A Klacko is a measure of weight equivalent to 2.729411 Femerons. The mass of an item in relationship to its molecular makeup. This number is vital for use in the Laser Particle Transporter's breakdown and reassembly of human cells.

# Chapter Three
## Houston, We Have a Problem

Downtown, in the Femeron capital city there is a park with gardens and fountains in front of a modern skyscraper. Females, alone or in groups are walking through the park. Most are wearing pant suits of similar design and style but a few are dressed in multiple skirts and blouses as was Ceena. Almost all of the females have bright colors dyed into their hair, either in streaks and highlights or their entire head. The women greet each other in passing. Some of the females stop and chat in groups with their friends. In the street, sleek autos run silently by. They have no tires or wheels but are powered by magnetic force. The roadbed having been imbedded with iron rails that are negatively charged, these rails repulse the negative side of magnets on the underbelly of the cars. The magnetic repulsion lifts the cars up and moves them silently forward down the street.

Dr. Joy walks up the wide front steps of the tall building and goes through the automatic doors and into the lobby on the first floor. At an elevator bank, she stands for a moment while the security computer acknowledges her identity. Green and white lights go on and the elevator door opens for her.

In the middle of the elevator is a large, padded chair. She sits in it and straps a seat belt on. The door closes and lights on the wall do a short count down; orange lights 5-4-3, red lights 2-1. The super elevator roars off up the shaft of the building. In a moment it is at full speed then begins to slow and comes to a complete stop with a soft 'bong' sound. The door opens and she unbuckles herself and steps out into the hallway. She turns right and continues down the hallway until she comes up to a strong energy force field blocking her way. She sees visible waves of current flowing from floor to ceiling across the width of the hallway. She passes her right hand across the front of a small panel on the wall and the energy screen loses its power.

Continuing down to the end of the hallway, she stops once again to identify herself. The door slides open and she enters into a brightly lit conference room. Large floor to ceiling windows provides a dramatic view of the nearby downtown skyscrapers. In the middle of the room there is a long conference table with high tech chairs. Each of the chairs have their own built-in computer console and keyboards. Other females are already in the room and are talking among themselves. As Dr. Joy looks around as her two female aids, Lolan 11 and Neera approach her with a third female.

"Dr. Joy," Lolan says. "I would like to introduce you to Chairperson Jemele. Chairperson, Dr. Joy."

"Nice to meet you. I've read so much about you and your work," Chairperson Jemele says, shaking hands with Dr. Joy.

"Thank you," Dr. Joy responds.

Turning to the other females, Chairperson Jemele calls out, "Shall we take our seats please?"

The women continue chatting as they walk to their places. Dr. Joy walks with her two aides to their assigned seats.

"What have you heard?" She asks Neera. She is a young woman with green hair.

"It doesn't look very promising," Neera answers in a low whisper. "All the members that I've spoken with, none thought you had any chance at all."

"Same with the ones I've spoken to," Lolan says. "To be honest, Dr. Joy, they were very negative. They suggested to me that you risk losing your funding and research credentials by making your recommendations public."

Dr. Joy shakes her head but smiles, "They're motivated purely by their love for me I'm sure."

"Don't be so sure," Neera says.

Dr. Joy glances at her as they take their seats.

"I must place before them what I believe to be the truth." Dr. Joy, turns to look into the eyes of her two assistants. "Are you still with me?"

"Of course." They both nod.

"Absolutely," the Lolan says and they both hug her.

"Okay then," Dr. Joy says. "Let's see if we can convince them."

The three women take their seats and in a few moments the chatter is stilled as Chairperson Jemele knocks on the glass top of the conference room table. She calls them to order and looks around the room before speaking. She is in her late fifties and has a well-groomed appearance. Her voice is strong. "I would like to welcome you all to the fourth meeting in our preparation for the upcoming Femeron Council Summit. At which a decision will have to be made as to how to address the current cloning crisis. Have we all agreed, that we must call this a crisis?"

Jemele sees that there is a general agreement among the participants around the table. "What we have learned so far," she continues, "is that there are alarming rates of failures at our cloning facilities and that these rates are climbing. We meet here today to reach an agreement on the options our Femeron leaders will have to choose from to address this crisis."

Chairperson Jemele pauses to see if there are any objections to her summary of the situation. There being none, she continues. "Our first step then will be to give the members of the Femeron Council an idea as to what the crisis is all about. After that, we must present them with their options. To help us with these final preparations, we have joining us today seven top genetics scientist." Jemele nods hello to the guest scientists. "I understand that Mala19 has worked on this portion of the presentation. Mala if you will, please."

A female stands up and takes a short bow as display screens light up around the room.

"The crisis in the cloning program is the result of a phenomenon which occurs in the chromosomes of a fertilized ovum cell." As Mala19 speaks, pictures and diagrams appear on the telescreens. "The cloning process uses an ovum which is extracted from a female and placed into a specially prepared culture. Here, both the fertilization of the egg and the initial maturation process takes place." Mala pauses and allows the images on the screen to illustrate her words. "This fertilization takes place when another female cell is introduced into the ovum. Once this introduction occurs, the division of cells within the ovum begins."

The display changes as Mala's discussion continues. "During the first phase of meiosis, the chromosomes from the donor and the recipient align to each other so they may swap genetic material. This exchange of genes is the basis of reproductive chemistry."

The other females nod their heads in understanding.

"But lots of things can happen in the process," Mala continues. "For example, portions of the sequence of the genes may not line up and so cannot be decoded. In extreme cases, the bases of some of the genes can form two connections to different, nearby genes. All in all, it is a very messy system whose only saving grace perhaps is that when it doesn't work, the faulty product is discarded. The point is, the rate of failure in our cloning process has reached crisis proportions and we must do something about it."

"If I may, Ms. Chairperson," another guest scientist interrupts Mala's presentation.

"Yes, Dr. Chen, please," Jemele says.

"You must remember," Dr. Chen stands as she addresses the conference room. "That the purpose of our cloning only female genes, was to remove the male's Y gene from the equation. The idea behind that being that if the deficient Y gene was not present in the reproduction process, then none of their negative traits would be present in the children conceived through cloning."

"Very true," Mala says. "Normally, when female X genes are introduced into the ovum, they unite with the X genes present in the recipient's ovum and there begins the creation of a fetus. One that will have the genetic makeup of all X-X genes. However, and here is where our problem lies, there is the possibility of an ovum creating a triple X gene. The fetus of this X-X-X gene, sadly, always develops into a hopelessly mutated being. If allowed to develop, and very few can in fact develop because some of their vital organs do not function so they do not survive, but if they did survive, these mutated babies would be horrible deformed."

"The possibility of a triple base forming from an X gene has always been such a statistical rarity." Mala points to the telescreen which shows an illustration of a chromosome and the genes attached to it. "In the past less than one tenth of one percent of genes formed this triple base. Within the past year, however, we've seen this rate of failure rise to over eleven percent! And our statistical research shows us that this rate is continuing to increase. As it stands now, with the present rate of occurrences, all cloning programs will have to be shut down within three to six months. That doesn't give us much time to find a solution."

"No, not much time at all," Chairperson Jemele interjects. "But Mala, I'm a bit confused with your presentation. If I am hearing you right, you are saying that in some instances X+X = 3X. That is like saying that one plus one equals three! How is that possible, I don't get it."

"Exactly right," Mala nods her head. "Nobody gets it. We're all wondering how that's possible. But it is happening. We are observing it."

"I see, well thank you, Mala. I'm clearer on it now. And yes, something must be done and that something is up to us to recommend to the summit council."

There is light applause for Mala and she acknowledges it with a bow of her head as she retakes her seat.

"At this point in our presentation," Jemele continues, "I would like to invite another of our genetics scientists to share us with their recommendations. Dr. Cassandra, would you please?"

Dr. Cassandra is a large middle-aged female. She stands and takes a quick bow then retakes her seat.

"Our work," she begins while adjusting her console screen, "has led us to conclude that the problem lies in the culture solution. Impregnated ovums are placed into a complex solution that mimics the characteristics of the uterus. Computer analysis has not yet pinpointed the exact chemical problem but we are continuing to vigorously search for it and we feel certain that we are narrowing down the possibilities. Therefore, it is our recommendation that the best course of action at this time would be to have an immediate, exponential increase in research. Including the creation of a central scientific committee whose function would be to oversee the use of those funds."

"And if the council authorized these additional expenditures?" Jamele asks. "What would be the estimated time before final results are obtained?"

Somewhat sheepishly, Dr. Cassandra admits, "I can't give you that estimate. We just don't know."

"I see," Chairperson Jamele nods.

"If I may," another female at the table stands.

"The chair recognizes, Dr. Sue Wee."

"Our studies show that Dr. Cassandra's work may lead to the discovery of what is causing this triple X gene, however what seems more likely, her research will lead to *nothing*."

The room buzzes with chatter as the females respond to her emphasis on the word, nothing.

Dr. Cassandra's face is flush with color as she is stung by the rebuke and criticism of her work.

"We respect her opinion of course," Dr. Sue Wee tries to placate Dr. Cassandra, "but the point is, she is making a guess. To tie up all or even most of the available research facilities and having them all focusing their work on just the culture would be unwise. Our team recommends that the council be asked to expand all research facilities and that these new facilities be divided up so they search in as many different areas as possible. Rather than to tie up all of the labs in searching in only one or two areas."

"I see," Chairperson Jamele says. "That does make sense."

"After all," Dr. Chen interjects, "we are all just guessing where to look."

The representatives break out in loud discussions.

Dr. Joy for her part, waits for the commotion to abate, looks to her two assistants, takes a deep breath and nods her head. "Well, this is it," she says. "Here we go."

Lolan and Neera nod affirmatively back to her. She stands and addresses the chair.

"May I?" she asks as she catches Chairperson Jemele's eye.

"The Chair recognizes, Dr. Joy."

Dr. Joy leaves her place and begins a leisurely stroll around the conference table. Although the room is still a buzz in conversations, she starts. "If I might." Her strong voice causes the murmuring to decrease.

"What you say, Dr. Chen is partly true," she looks Dr. Chen in the eye. "We *are* all guessing as to what is the cause of the triple X phenomenon. There is one solution, however, that would solve the crisis *immediately*."

Dr. Joy pauses to gather her thoughts. She considers her words. "If we used male sperm in fertilization, there would be absolutely no chance of the triple X chromosome occurring in the fetus' cells."

Dr. Joy's statement is met with an uproar which only abates as the Chair calls for order. Before Dr. Joy can continue, another female vehemently calls out, "This is absurd! You're suggesting that we reinstate the male Y gene back into the general population. Your plan may rid us of the triple X problem, sure, but at what cost?"

Another female just as loud, "Might I remind Dr. Joy that we are an *advanced* civilization. What she proposes is to step back into the age of War!"

Another shouts, "Really! We might as well try *anything* else before we turn the playgroups loose!"

Dr. Joy points to this female, "No, you're wrong. We don't have to use every male. We can choose only those males that have developed, emotionally and psychologically. Only males that have shown this advancement through observations and testing. We introduce only the best into our breeding programs."

"Do you suggest, Dr. Joy," Dr, Chen asks in a calm voice, "that there are males who have developed psychologically? Males *dependable* enough for us to create our future generations with?"

Dr. Joy smiles. "Yes. We only need a few thousand and with our many different ovum's, we could produce an almost infinite number of offspring without ever inbreeding."

Dr. Cassandra smirking, "Show us *one* male worthy of what you suggest."

"She can't!" another interrupts. "She can't show you one, no less a few thousand!"

"If I could show you one," Dr. Joy argues, "would you agree?"

Before Dr. Cassandra can answer another says, "I think we have wasted enough time on this. I propose that we vote on Dr. Joy's, uh..well, her suggestion. Let's vote so we can move on."

The other females agree including Chairperson Jamele. She taps the conference table with her finger to get their attention and says, "All in favor of Dr. Joy's proposal?"

Looking around the table she sees, as does Dr. Joy that there are no hands raised. The Chair looks at Dr. Joy with a touch of sadness as it is plain to see that she has convinced no one of accepting her radical plan.

The meeting continues as Dr. Joy and her two assistants walk toward the door. Their eyes meet, Dr. Joy is calm and confident. They speak softly as the conference continues on behind them, a soft murmur of voices as they open the door and exit.

"I must leave," she tells them in the hallway, "but I want you two to stay. I want to know their final decision. The details of the solution that they will present at the Femeron General Council."

"Where will you be, doctor?" Neera asks.

"I'm going to the mountains to speak with Milon." She squeezes their hands and says warmly. "We'll show them a male they've never imagined existed."

They hug, touch cheeks and Dr. Joy turns and walks down the hall as the assistants go back into the conference room.

Dr. Joy takes the elevator to the top floor where she enters into an office with a sign on its door; Laser Particle Transporter-Long Shots

The room is filled with wall to wall control panels and computers. At the far end of the room, an opening into a tunnel. It looks like the laser transporter in Lolan 11's room but much bigger and many times more powerful.

# Chapter Four
## We're Looking for a Few Good Men

The receptionist is a tall, beautiful woman with long legs and auburn hair with a tint of blonde highlights. After checking Dr. Joy's travel authorizations, she asks, "Destination?"

"Authorized travel to Helene Mountains."

"Do you have the exact coordinates?"

"Umm," Dr. Joy looks up as if that might help her memory. "Let's see. I not sure if this is exact but I believe it's 152 degrees, slope 481, duration 291."

The receptionist gets up from behind the glass reception desk and walks towards the bank of computers on the wall behind her. "Better let's check. If we are off by even a few hundreds of a second, many vital parts of you will end up missing."

"Right." Joy nods, "need to avoid that."

They both laugh and walk together towards one of the lighted panels on the wall. The receptionist extracts the necessary data but as they turn to walk back to her desk, they are startled by a sudden crash. Dr. Joy turns toward the far bank of mainframe computers where she heard the loud noise. She walks over and peers around the corner and sees on the other side a male laying sprawled out on the floor. He's lying in a heap. The male is in his forties. He has a touch of grey in his hair and is chubby.

Dr. Joy has a surprised, puzzled expression, as she helps him up. The receptionist is close behind her and says. "Oh no, no, no! I can't believe you did that!"

"Damn wiring shocked the hell out of me," he says, brushing himself off. "I'm okay though. Don't you worry about me. Nope. Thanks, thanks," he says as the two women help him up.

Before Dr. Joy can even ask what he is doing there, the receptionist says hurriedly, "I can explain. You see this male was sent here to...uh..uh..to fix-the-computer- switches.

She pauses, thinks, then, "He's being trained for computer technology." She pauses again and says in a slower manner, as she tries to make her story believable. "It's part of a *new* program, just started. Very, *very* new. You probably haven't even heard of it yet. Ha Ha Ha."

As the receptionist is speaking, she continues to straighten out his clothes. They both are looking Dr. Joy in the eye to see if she's buying it. The chubby male becomes annoyed at the receptionist's constant pulling on his shirt and he pushes her hands away just as she releases her grip. The force of his unhindered shove propels him forward and into Dr. Joy's as she is only a foot away. He stumbles and ends up with his head and both hands on her breasts.

The receptionist looks at the ceiling and more to herself, "Why me?"

The force of the momentum has thrown Dr. Joy back against another bank of computers. Her butt accidently hits the controls and the lighting system begins to go on and off in sections across the room.

The three of them stand for a moment looking around at the ceiling. The male still has his head half buried in Dr. Joy's breasts but he straightens up with a little help from the receptionist. The lights above their heads are still going off and on and some sections are blinking in rotation. Dr. Joy turns to see which of the buttons she's accidently hit. As she turns and bends over to read the control panel, both the receptionist and the male also bend over to look at the controls. Their heads collide with the doctor's butt. They all three, stand straight up and Dr. Joy laughs. Rita studies her face, then joins in the laughter. Still laughing, and with the lights still going on and off, Dr. Joy holds both of her palms out towards them and says, "Don't Move!"

She checks to make certain they aren't going to crash into her again, turns back to the panel and finds the switch to bring the lights back under control.

"There," she says turning back to face Rita and the male. "That was very interesting." "I had fun," he says.

"I hope we didn't short circuit the entire building," the receptionist says.

"Now what were you explaining about a new program?" Dr. Joy asks.

"Well, ah, uh," the receptionist stammers.

"No, no, no," the male wags his finger. "No use lying about it. We're doing what we want, right?" Rita nods, yes.

He turns to Dr. Joy and explains, "I've escaped from my playgroup. I was hiding here, trying to figure a way to escape through the LPT, to get really far away but before I could figure out how to work the transporter, Rita-nine found me."

"I guess I broke the rules," Rita says, "but we've been having so much fun together. Louwee's not like any of the other male that I've met before." She pauses and looks at Dr. Joy. "You won't understand but I love him. I want to enjoy his company. We don't do anyone any harm. With the other males it's like…like, well, it's like they're crazy or something but Louwee, he's different."

"I know exactly what you mean," Dr. Joy says. "I know some males who are 'different' too."

"Really?" Rita asks, hopeful that Dr. Joy might not turn Louwee into the authorities.

"Yes, really. I'm Dr. Joy, but please call me Joy." She reaches out and shakes their hands. "Listen, I must be on my way but when I return, I want you both to go to my mountain retreat." She pauses, looks at them and says, "You'll be safe there and I know it's something you'll both enjoy."

Rita hugs Joy, she's near tears. "C'mon let's get you out there."

They all three go back to the front office and walk to the LPT in the corner of the room. Louwee stops next to Rita at the control panel but Joy keeps walking towards the LPT opening. She turns and asks excitedly, "Wait, please, you must tell me if you know any more men like Lou who are, you know, different? Of course, you must know many others! You've been living in playgroups your entire life."

Rita and Lou look at each other. There is some doubt whether they should respond or not. Their faces show their hesitation and Joy sees their concern. She understands, after all she could be planning to set them and their friends up. "I know how you feel and what you're thinking." She looks squarely into their faces as she asks. "Would you take a chance and trust me if you knew that my friends and I have been working to free men like Louwee from the playgroups?"

Rita and Louwee remain doubtful and say nothing.

"I'm telling you the truth and pretty soon our moment will be at hand. When it comes, we'll need help to convince the Femeron leaders that some males should not be locked away. That some of them find the playgroups a prison and yet they live, even in these prisons, free from games. Do you understand? If you know any of these men or if you know people who might, it could make a difference whether our plans succeed or fail."

Joy pauses and looks at Lou. He remains expressionless but there is understanding in his eyes. Joy sees this in him and says, "Think about it. We'll talk again when I return."

She turns towards the LPT. Rita inputs the coordinates and the LPT Longshot machine kicks in. It is a monstrous, powerful thing. Tremendous energy is released as bright bands of laser lights rip through the opening of the LPT. The sound produced is a low, rumbling which moves the room with its power.

Rita, loudly so as to be heard over the machine, "Okay, we're ready."

Dr. Joy turns around, "Oh, I almost forgot. What hours do you run the LPT?"

"Why do you want to know?" Rita asks and Dr. Joy is taken back. Her expression changes. She is annoyed but says calmly and smiles, "Because I may be bringing someone back with me. I don't want him seen, especially by people I can't trust." Rita reflects on Joy's statement then says, "Call me whenever you're ready and I'll be here for your return."

Joy looks at Rita, nods her head affirmatively and smiles. She knows that Rita at least is willing to see things as they develop. It's the most Joy could ask of her at this point.

"Thanks, see ya."

With this she turns and steps into the bands of lights. Her body disappears as it passes into the laser field. The sound gets louder, more powerful as the LPT reaches its full potential.

When Dr. Joy is gone, at that last instant, outside the building, with the city in the background, a brilliant flash of light streaks out from the top of the skyscraper towards the mountains in the far distance.

# Chapter Five
## Innocence of a Child

The laser beam flashes over of the city and across open plains to the mountain range in the distance. The beam lands exactly in the opening of a Laser Particle Receiver, an LPR unit, situated on the outside deck of a Spanish style estate. The laser light strikes the LPR and Dr. Joy steps out of the light band by completing the step she began far away in Femeron City.

After she touches down and walks out onto the patio deck, a trailing band of light flows into the LPR. It is much less dense and quickly fades out. The climax of energy from the sight and sounds of this 'Long Shot' journey dissolves into a quiet country setting. Birds are chirping and somewhere off in the distance, a dog is barking. Dr. Joy stands for a moment with both hands on the top rail of the patio's wall looking out over the hillside. The estate is half way up the mountain. Mesquite trees and bushes intermingle with the long, yellow grasses on the steep hillside. A paved two lane road winds up the hill and she can make out several of the neighbors' roofs and swimming pools.

She walks across the slate-tiled patio and enters the hacienda through double French doors. She pauses for a moment to look into the living room. A white shag throw carpet partially covers dark wood floors. Large cushioned chairs and couches surround a wooden coffee table. Behind the couch, a stone fireplace and mantel take up the center of a long wall. On either side of the fireplace, oil paintings hang in simple frames. The paintings are abstract in bold, bright colors. In the corners of the room, plants hang in macramé holders from the high, open beam rafters. Other larger plants are in tall clay pots. Looking out of the living room windows to her left, she sees the other half of the outside patio. She goes out through another set of double French doors and stands at the waist high stone patio wall looking down to a lush flower garden. To the right, outside a bedroom on the bottom floor, an area in the garden has been made into an outdoor sculpture studio. A tall block of marble stands secured to the wood floor. It appears only half-finished but Dr. Joy can make out the figures of a man, a child and a large cat. A leopard?

She smiles down at a male as he chisels patiently but he is so engrossed in his work; he doesn't notice her. She has to call to him twice. The second time louder, "Milon."

He turns and looks up and it takes a moment before he recognizes her.

"Joy!" he shouts. He puts down his hammer and chisel and walks briskly to the stone steps. Joy walks down and they meet on the steps half way up and hug and kiss.

"What a great surprise! It's not that I didn't recognize you," he explains as they hold each other at arms' length. "I was still envisioning the completed work and really, I didn't see anything for a moment. But you brought me back to the present and how wonderful it is to see you!"

Milon is dressed in loose fitting clothes. He has on sneakers and an old, wrinkled shirt. The shirt is covered in thick stone dust so that its print of colorful flowers can barely be made out. The marble dust coats him from head to foot. His black curly hair is white with it. Joy's cheeks and the front of her clothes are now also smudged white. She looks down at herself, back to Milon and laughs.

"Milon you don't sculpt the marble, you eat it! You breathe it! You probably shit it!" They both laugh.

"You're right about that," he says. "There's nothing about the marble that I don't love. Nothing in this world makes me feel better than to chisel it. I love to feel it's solidness through my hands. To feel its hidden resiliency." Milon pauses to search for words. Then adds, "In my mind I can see the figure trapped within and I have to plan and work bit by bit to release it from the stone."

"It's beautiful," Joy says as they come to the bottom of the stairs and stand in front of the sculpture.

She walks around the large marble block as Milon sits at a small table and follows her with his eyes.

"The figures are emerging, feature by feature from the almost jewel like stone," Joy describes the sculpture as she slides her hand over its surface. "I see a man with his arm on a child's shoulder. This is a leopard lying down next to them?"

"Yes, a leopard," Milon agrees.

"It's magnificent. I like the alert expression on its face. The child's expression too, shows the innocence of youth. But tell me, is it a boy or girl?" "It's both, or neither, as only a child can be."

"Yes, I see," Joy says. "And the old man, I love his expression, calm, patient. His bearing is humble yet he stands straight and unbent under his years. You've shown us an obviously powerful body beneath his robe." Dr. Joy points to the outline of a bicep muscle, "but his arm lies gently around the child's shoulder. They are both looking to something out in the distance. The leopard is looking at it too and somehow... I don't know... I get the feeling that they all three are ready to greet someone. Yes, it's like someone is approaching and they are about to move. It sends a chill up my spine."

She walks over to the table and chair and bends down and kisses Milon on the forehead then on his lips. She sits in his lap and places her cheek to his and puts an arm around his neck. She closes her eyes in contentment. He holds her comfortably as they both look back at the unfinished statue.

"It's alive!" she says. "I keep seeing them move."

"They're becoming," he says.

"Yes, that's it. Even their expressions somehow keep changing. They look like they're smiling then like they're staring off into the distance. Then their faces change to a look of recognition, then back to smiling."

"We're all just becoming," Milon adds.

"Yes," Joy agrees.

After a pause, still considering the sculpture, "What do they symbolize? Why an old man, a child and a leopard?"

"They are all part of the same soul," Milon explains. "Different natures of the same spirit."

"I'm not sure I understand," she says.

Milon searches for the words. "We're all part of the same soul; different leaves on the same tree."

"And where are we headed? What is our destiny?"

"Total awareness, I think. Or at least total empathy." Milon yawns as he says this last part.

"When was the last time you slept?" Dr. Joy asks.

"Hmm, I don't remember was that this morning or yesterday?"

"And you probably haven't eaten well either."

"I had fruit and coffee."

Joy smiles and hugs him, "I'm going to make us a nice dinner."

"That would be great, thank you."

She takes his hand and they walk back up the stairs to the patio. In the kitchen she starts to search for what food is available. He goes to help and she wags her finger.

"You go shower, change and lie down. I'll call you when it's ready. If you fall sleep, don't worry. We'll eat when you wake up."

He nods, kisses her and leaves the kitchen and goes into a large, white room. Presumably the bathroom, although there are no toilets or sinks. He disrobes and steps into an open shower. Inputting instructions onto a control panel, the shower emits harmonious sound waves that he steps into. The waves shake off all of the marble dust. Even his hair is spotlessly cleaned without water. The sounds are low toned and their forceful humming and the fine acoustics of the shower area, create a tingling of excitement.

After changing into casual clothes, he thinks about lying down but wants to be near her and returns to the kitchen.

"I couldn't sleep knowing that you were out here. I haven't seen you in, what, six weeks?"

"Not quite, five."

"Yes, well, I am excited to see you. You look wonderful."

"Thank you," she turns to him and smiles. They hug and kiss.

"I was just thinking about when I first met you," Joy looks over as she chops vegetables on the cutting board. "Do you remember?"

"Oh yes," he laughs. "I was carving figures into the walls outside of a playgroup. The authorities told me that if I didn't stop, I would be sent to a maximum-security group. They were going to put me through 'Habit Uniform-Reform Treatment' or what the boys liked to call 'HURT.'"

"Yes, I remember," Joy continues to prepare the meal, working on the salad and making the dressing with fresh limes. She looks up at him. "They called me in to do an evaluation and you brought me outside and showed me the sculptures you had banged into the cement walls."

"And you liked them!" Milon laughs.

"Oh, yes, I did. *Loved* them."

"And you promised me a block of stone to work on."

"You will never know what I went through trying to convince the guards that it was okay for them to allow a 200-kilo boulder into the facility."

"For medicinal purposes, right?" Milon says and they both laugh.

"Well, they weren't happy but they were sick and tired of you chipping away the outside walls, so they finally let me bring it in."

"You brought me real tools too," Milon smiles at the memory. "Hammer and chisels and finishing stones. Geez I was happy. It was the first time I had the right implements to work with."

"You glowed from within," Joy agrees. "When I saw your completed work, a fantastic sculpture of birds on tree branches, I knew I had to get you your freedom"

"That was two years ago."

"You've come a long way since then."

They carry their plates over to a glass and metal table by the window in the kitchen.

"Yes, well, I'm still becoming but it is much easier being free to work and live."

They divide up the salad and he pours them each a glass of white wine.

"I agree, in fact that's part of the reason why I've come to see you."

"Why is that?"

Joy clinks glasses with him and takes a slow sip of her wine and thinks before explaining.

"We've a plan to gain the freedom for all the men who are ready for it."

"Who's we?"

"There are many females who feel the way you and I do and now is the time. We have the opportunity to do something about it."

Her voice has gained a stronger emotional tone and she catches herself becoming too strong, too fast. She pauses to regain her control and looks into Milon's eyes. Her lover, her friend. He is so many things to her. She finds it difficult to explain. Was it fair to ask him to risk losing his own freedom for the hope that they could help others? Would he think she had done all this for him just to set him up? To use him? What he owed her was honesty, not sacrifices. She had said this more than once and now she was asking him to sacrifice.

"The time has come," she says, breaking the silence in a gentle voice. "The scene is set. All we have to do is play it right. Our chances may never be this good again."

"I don't understand." Milon puts down his glass. "This good again for what? What do I have to do with your plan?"

"We need you. We need you to come back to the city and to meet with Femeron leaders."

Milon makes a face then says sarcastically, "Sure, I'll talk them right into it. Anything else you want me to have them do? I mean while I'm at it."

"Don't be sarcastic," she frowns.

"No?" Milon snaps back. "What should I be, grateful? I mean you're giving me the opportunity to have myself arrested and thrown back in the looney bin."

"Actually, yes," she says.

"Thanks, but no thanks, darling," he toasts her with his wine glass and takes a sip.

"You can do it. I know you can," she smiles and tries to stay upbeat.

"Look, I'm no politician."

"I'm not asking you to be one, either."

"No? What are you asking me to be then?" His tone reflects his impatience with the discussion.

"You know, you remind me of Steve McQueen when you get angry."

"I'm not angry," he objects, "and you've been watching too many ancient movies."

"Perhaps," she nods. "I like their rough style."

"I don't want to ruin what I have," he says looking into his wine glass.

"No, of course not and I can't promise how this will turn out, but listen I do promise you this. I will get you back here and free again."

"Yeah?" Milon shakes his head. "They might have a thing or two to say about that. Don't you think?"

"Yes, there'll be some women that we'll have to overcome, but I got you free once and I will do what I have to. You won't end up in a playgroup."

He stops to think. "So, I meet with some Femeron leaders, then what?"

"Just be you, that's all. I know you and I know them. If anyone can get through to them." Her words hang in the air. Neither of them speaks, both are thinking, trying to understand all of the ramifications.

"After the meeting," Dr. Joy continues, "they will agree with us that some males are capable of psychological and emotional growth."

"Well, gee, thanks."

"Would I lie to you?" she asks with a laugh.

He looks at her goes to answer then ignores it and asks instead, "Then what? If they agree with you that I'm *evolved*, what would happen then?"

"Then we present other evolved males. Over time we will get them released from the playgroups."

"Their prisons," he interjects.

"Yes, their prisons and let them join us in society."

"Their own apartments? Their own free lives?"

She nods, yes.

"Sounds good," he says.

"It does, doesn't it?"

"And I'm the shining example for them, huh?" He shakes his head and purposely drops both his knife and fork on the table. "Listen," he says as he stands up, "I'm not into freeing anyone but myself. Can you understand that?"

"Sure, I can understand it," she stands too. "But to be honest, I don't agree with it."

"No, you wouldn't. Listen, I am so very grateful for you and what you have done for me but I am not free inside. I worry all the time about what happens if they find me? This is in my mind, all the time. So, I'm not really free, am I? And I don't want to risk losing what I have."

"Of course not," Joy holds both his hands and he doesn't pull away. "I understand and I worry about the same thing but by saving others, you would be saving yourself too. Right now, you are a fugitive. How great would it be to be legal? Huh? Not worried about the authorities?"

"And if I don't cooperate, you would turn me in?"

"Of course not!" Joy is angry now. She lets go of his hands. Then calmer, "No, of course not, Milon."

She folds her arms. "Think of the other men who would love to be free? Free from their lives of insane captivity? Think for a minute of the children who are destined for wasted lives within the playgroups. Can't you see that you will be saving other artists? There are writers, poets; people with great talent. Artists who will never be nurtured and encouraged." She looks into his eyes for a long moment. "What about those souls?"

He hesitates. "I'm not here to save anyone."

"That's just what I would expect of a male," Joy's anger shows again. "Maybe I was wrong! Maybe there is no hope for your sex!"

Milon studies her. He takes a few moments to think and analyze. "You're not wrong," he says. "I think your idea is right, your plan is great. It's just that I'm not the right person for it."

"Maybe you're not," she says in a calm tone once again, "but we can't wait for the perfect person. We have to do this now. There's a lot going on that you're not aware of. We have to go with what we've got."

They stand in silence. Milon walks back to the table and sits down. She follows him and they both pick at their food.

"I don't want to confront the Femeron culture," he finally says.

"Sure, right. Why should you? *You're* safe, right here, removed from all the problems, far from the injustices. Well, okay then, stay." She takes a long pull on the wine. "Tell you this though," she says as she places the wine glass back on the table setting. "You will have no peace as long as the problems remain unresolved."

"Yes, I see that too," he agrees. "I understand what you're saying. I have an obligation, but I just don't think...I don't know how I'm to accomplish it."

"I still love you," she says. "I know that you have to do what you feel is right for you. I wish you could see that this is right for you."

"I'm not sure what is right anymore." He shrugs his shoulders. "I know what you've said is true. Look, I'll help you in any way I can. Isn't there another job where I don't have to talk to the Femeron chiefs?"

"You're frightened," Joy says.

"No, not frightened I...," Milon is about to defend himself but stops. His head is down but now he lifts it and looks back at Joy. "Okay, yeah. It does frighten me," he considers it even more. "Umm...okay, yes," he nods, "Yeah, 'frightened' describes it."

"I love it when you're sense of humor shows," Joy says. "It gives you balance. It does. And with your joker's eye, you can laugh and that centers you and because of it, others can see the lightness in your soul."

"What you need here is a Hero, not a Joker." She laughs.

"No, really," Milon says. "Someone who will go in there and look them in the eye and tell them how it's going to be. Take it or leave it. Final offer. That sort of thing."

Joy laughs.

He smiles. "No, huh? A little too direct?"

She is still laughing.

"Okay, I'm not kidding, you need to find someone else who isn't afraid of them. No lie, I'm telling you the truth, I don't like them and I'm worried how I will sound. What I'll say. I'm scared alright and there's no way I can hide it from them."

"And you don't have to hide it. It doesn't matter. You can feel frightened or angry or happy. That's the point. I only want you to be you."

"As you put me on display."

"Screw that! We're going to show the Femerinians that in spite of what they've done to you, you are still their equal. You believe that, don't you?"

"Of course," Milon says, then ponders. "Femerinians huh?" he smiles.

"Yes," Joy laughs at the word too. "Femerinians. And now is the time to prove it." She smiles and he nods his head in agreement.

***

The next morning, Dr. Joy is standing by the Laser Particle Transporter. "Milon," she calls into the house. "It's time."

"Okay, here we go," he says as he comes out and stands with her.

Dr. Joy inputs the coordinates into the control panel, then speaks into her watch.

"Receiving unit 8969 calling LPT main control."

"Hi, Dr. Joy. We're ready when you are."

"Thanks, Rita. Send her."

The control panel at the ranch's LPT lights up and a laser beam can be seen as it comes over the mountains and into the receiving unit. The beam is humming with energy. The interior is bright with lights. Dr. Joy waits for Milon. He steps into the laser beam and is gone. She speaks into her watch phone.

"How'd he do?"

"Great, safe and sound."

"Ready for me?" she asks.

"Yes, all clear for transport."

Dr. Joy steps into the laser lights and is gone.

# Chapter Six
## What's the Plan?

Several days later, Dr. Joy and Milon are sitting in her living room in a high-rise apartment building. The computer announces, "Paula Fourteen, Representative District five, Femeron, Capital City."

"Allow access," Joy says and looks over at Milon. He looks serious but she smiles at him, "Well, here we go."

They watch the telescreen as it shows a young woman, entering the elevator. Then exiting on their floor.

"At least she didn't bring guards with her," Milon jokes.

"C'mon, these females are on our side, *your* side, I should say."

She opens the sliding front door and greets Paula as she walks down the hallway.

"Come in, come in. I've been waiting for you," Joy gives her a hug and they touch cheeks. The door whooshes closed behind them. Joy gestures with an open hand to Milon, "May I introduce you to Milon. Milon, this is Paula. Paula is the representative for our district here in Femeron City."

"How do you do?" Milon walks to her and offers his hand.

She takes it and they politely shake.

"All goes well for me," Paula says. "And for you?"

"Yes, well, everything was going great until I got talked into this little adventure here."

"Please, take a seat," Paula gestures to the couch and chairs.

Joy and Milon sit next to each other on the couch and Paula across from them on a large, overstuffed chair.

"This is a special occasion for me, Milon," Paula breaks the silence.

"Oh, yes?" Milon asks.

"Yes, most definitely. You see Joy has spoken of you many times. I feel I know you."

"Spoken of me, huh. I had no idea." Milon gives Joy a stare. "You mean you knew I was outside the playgroup?"

"Yes, everything," Paula says.

"We never discussed this," Milon looks to Joy again. Then back to Paula. I didn't realize that anyone else was aware of my refuge."

"Excellent choice of words," Joy says.

"Obviously I did not disapprove," Paula points out.

"No, I guess you didn't. Thank you for that." Milon looks to Joy then back to Paula.

"So, I am to convince you that I am human. Right now, that seems absurd to me."

"Absurd?" Paula asks.

"Not absurd that I'm human, but absurd that I should have to even discuss it."

"I understand," Paula nods. "Perhaps the better question would be, do you feel you are my equal?"

"Yes, I feel equal to you," Milon says.

"Bland," Paula comments.

"What?"

"I said, bland. There's a difference you know between being gentle and being timid."

"Okay, fair enough," Milon says. "And here's what I really feel. The question I want to know is whether *you* think you are *my* equal?"

"Better," Paula says. "Before I answer that, may I ask you something?"

"Certainly. Have at it."

Paula gets up and walks across the apartment. She has unbuttoned the top four buttons of her blouse exposing her breasts.

"Milon," she smiles at him, "do you feel desire for me? Would you like to touch me? Stroke my body with your hands? It's okay with Joy. We can go into the bedroom and have sex."

She bends over and exposes very nice breasts.

"No, not really," Milon says.

"No?"

"Sorry, no. You are an attractive female, don't get me wrong."

"And desirable?" Paula shakes loose her long, blonde hair and has a pout on her lips. "Please explain your lack of manliness."

"It's not a lack of manliness. Before I'm physically attracted to someone, I need to feel a closeness to them. Otherwise we're just strangers groping one another." He looks at her but she doesn't respond. "Of course, once I feel close with someone, physical love making is among my favorite preoccupations."

"And this emotional closeness?" Paula asks. "How do you find it? It seems like a long process."

"With some people it is, with others it happens right away."

"Go on," Paula motions with a nod of her head.

"Well, with some people there's an open, easy feeling from the start. I can feel a oneness very quickly with them."

"You don't feel that oneness with me?"

"Not right at the moment, no. Do you?"

Paula looks over to Joy. She smiles, looks back at Milon and says, "Yes, I do feel a oneness with both of you."

"Thank you," Milon says. "I am beginning to see myself in you too."

"Yes, Milon," Paula says, "I do believe we are equal."

Milon gets up from the couch and gives Paula a hug. After their embrace Paula suggests, "It's a balmy night outside. I feel like walking by the river. Would you two like join me?"

A flash of concern crosses Joy's face.

"It's late and he can wear a hat," Paula says. "There aren't many people around. It'll be safe."

Joy looks to Milon for his opinion. He responds with a smile and says, "Do you doubt the word of a Femeron government official?"

Then to Paula, "A flowing river sounds just the place to walk and talk."

"Let's hope we can find the right strategy to make this happen," Joy says as they head for the door.

Joy smiles to herself as they go out and down the hallway. She has witnessed Milon's spirit triumph. He reached into himself and found the strength to conquer his apprehensions. Joy feels his optimism. She sees him now as she always imagined he could be. His discussions about the natural laws of the universe and of the harmony of life, have real meaning as he puts those beliefs into action on life's stage.

"The right strategy?" Milon answers her.

"How about feel the vibes and go with the good ones?"

Joy nods. She sees his charisma. He is a burning power, steady and even. She knows now that whether or not they succeed, his charisma will have triumphed.

"Your song is a good one," she tells him.

"Goodness and peace shall overcome. The human race will sing a clear song; all we have to do is love one another." Milon says in a bright tone.

"Confidence and self-worth," Paula adds, "have no fear of the darkness. Your humor will respond to the threats. Humor may anger the powers that be, but it will unnerve them as well. Nothing speaks a person's self-confidence better than their ability to face apparent danger, physical or emotional, with a relaxed, funny response."

"So, that will be our strategy then? Comic responses, but done with self-confidence?" Joy asks.

"Got a better one?" Milon asks.

"Not really, no," she says.

"We need to decide the best way to play this," Paula speaks as they continue to walk along the riverside park. "Should we bring Milon to meet as many of the Femeron leaders as possible before the summit begins? Or else wait and introduce him to the entire summit assembly in the middle or at the end of the cloning debate?"

"We only have three days," Joy says. "How many leaders can we meet with in that short a time?"

"Quite a few actually," Paula says. "The key ones are in this capital and even those who are coming from distant places, they are in town already."

"Maybe a dozen or so?" Joy asks.

"Yes, I think." Paula continues. "Well, we'll meet as many as we can but it still leaves the big surprise presentation at the summit as the main play."

Milon jumps in front of the two females, "And now ladies, we are proud to present, Milon the Magnificent!"

They laugh at his characterization.

"Isn't he cute?" Joy jokes.

"And now that you've all seen him," Milon still pretending to address the summit assembly, "we ask you to free all the monkeys. Open all of the zoos and let these creatures roam among us once again."

"Doesn't sound too convincing," Joy acknowledges.

"Not exactly the scientific approach," Paula agrees. "But what else do we have?" They fall silent.

"You realize that it'll never work on just Milon's presence?" Paula looks to Joy as they walk on.

"I say we either find more males like Milon or else we find another way to do this. Perhaps even another time."

"How many more advanced males would we have to show them to make it work?" Joy asks.

"I don't know," Paula says, "four or five hundred? That might work, maybe."

Joy reflects on the number.

"Do you think you can bring us that many?" Paula asks Milon.

He doesn't answer.

"I know a few more," Dr. Joy thinks out loud. "My aides know of some others. Milon, you must know some too."

"Sure," Milon nods affirmatively. "Not five hundred but dozens."

"We may not be able to show up with five hundred on such short notice," Joy explains to Paula, "but if we can bring one hundred just from the local playgroups, won't that be proof enough that many others exist?"

"Seems logical to me. Yes, I think it would," Paula agrees.

They walked on for another minute in silent thought.

"Well, Paula?" Joy asks.

"Okay," Paula nods her head, "let's go with it."

"Good," Joy smiles at Milon, then to Paula, "We'll need a written order from you allowing us the authority to have these males released into our custody."

"Not a problem," Paula says. "In the meantime I will speak personally with some of the other Femeron leaders."

\*\*\*

The next morning, Dr. Joy is in a large conference room where she and her aides, Neera and Lolan along with Rita, Louis and Milon and a dozen other females are gathered. They are speaking among themselves and Dr. Joy has to clap several times to get their attention.

"Attention, attention, please."

The buzz in the room comes down and she continues.

"We will be passing out list of males and their playgroup locations. Our nine teams will then go out and bring those males that they have been assigned to secure."

Lolan and Neera go around the room handing out tiny disks.

"I wish you all luck and I will be checking in with you during the day." Dr. Joy smiles and gives a little hug to each person as they leave the room.

The conference room is theirs alone and Dr. Joy and Milon stand by the door.

"Our own assignment is a little tougher," she explains to him. "The two boyhood friends, Paul and Max that you've given me as recommendations, well come to find out that they're both being held in Maximum Security."

"Can't Paula get them moved to a regular playgroup?" Milon asks.

"No," she shakes her head, "there wasn't enough time to go through the whole process. They're still in Max Security."

"But we have the authority to bring them out. Based on Paula's written release, right?"

"Not exactly," Dr. Joy shakes her head again.

"Not exactly? Okay, then how *exactly* do we do this?"

"I have a plan to sneak them out."

"Oh, really? Sneak them out?"

"Yes, and it won't be easy so are you certain they're worth the effort? I mean, go over again why you selected them."

"Sure. Well, you see, I've known both of them, Paul and Max since we were little kids."

Milon smiles at the memory of their childhood but Dr. Joy slightly shakes her head in the negative.

"Being your friends doesn't make them useful or right for our project."

"No, it doesn't. That's what I was going to explain. You see Paul is the smartest guy I know. He reads everything and darn if he doesn't understand it all. If I ever had a question about anything; nature, physics, astronomy, history, politics. You name it. He's studied it and has a great way of sharing his knowledge. He's very well spoken."

"And Max?" Dr. Joy asks.

"Okay, well, Max. Yeah, Max" Milon nods his head. "Alright, you see the thing with Max is, is that he's tough. Any situation you're in, you can count on Max to have your back. Know what I mean?"

"I think so, but that doesn't really qualify him for this project. We're not looking for strong arms here. Strong minds. Strong personalities, sure. But..."

"Well here's the thing," Milon interrupts her. "You see it's exactly the strong-arm part that Paul will want if he's to go on this little journey with us."

"I see," Dr. Joy nods.

"Yes, so it's like a two for one deal. Look at it like that, you get two for one."

"And you don't think Paul will come with us without Max?'

"Yeah, no, that's not going to happen," Milon says.

"I see." Dr. Joy stops to consider. "Alright. Okay. I'll take your word for it. Let's do this."

She walks into the hallway and goes to close the door behind them. "I'll explain it all to you on our way over to the security prison."

"What do you mean, on *our* way over? I can't go into a maximum security pen." Milon has stopped walking. "You're not planning for me to go in there with you, are you?"

"Well, actually, yes. I'll need you with me." Dr. Joy puts a hand on his shoulder. "You see the other problem we have is I need both Paul and Max to cooperate with me. The last I heard they were not very trusting of females. I'll need you there to convince them it's safe."

Milon laughs. "And who's going to convince me?"

"Me, dear." Joy hugs, kisses and grinds on him.

# Chapter Seven
## You Want Me to Do What?

Lolan Eleven and Neera walk down the hallway of a male playgroup.

"She said, number six, right?" Lolan asks as they both look for numbers on the doors.

"Yes, number six." Neera walks ahead of her. "Okay, here it is, here."

Lolan taps the door with two quick knocks then opens it and goes in. She finds that they are interrupting a milking session where two pretty females are playing with a tall male while he is attached to a milking appliance.

"Sorry, to disturb you ladies," Lolan says. She points her chin at the male. "We have orders to bring this one up front."

"What, right now?" The male asks incredulous.

"Afraid so, Wally boy," Lolan says as Neera steps in and begins to unattach the collection tube and bottle.

"Now wait, wait just a minute," the male tries spinning around to avoid them. For all his effort, he is only getting wrapped up and tangled in the tube.

"Let them finish first, won't ja?" he pleads.

The four women are now all trying to un-tangle him.

"Okay, listen. Please, just another ten minutes," he tries to reason with them.

"Sorry, we're on a tight schedule," Neera says.

"You? What about *my* tight schedule?" He continues to hump through all of this. Knowing it's coming to an end, he gets aggressive and starts to feel up not just the two female milkers, but now Neera and Lolan as well.

The ladies enjoy being felt up and laugh and giggle.

"See, now isn't this fun?" he says.

"Gotta go, Buddy," Lolan insists.

"Alright, just *three* minutes more," he's humping now with his eyes closed trying to reach climax. "*Two* minutes then," he pleads as they finally pull him off. He humps his way out of the room and down the hallway, feeling them up as much as they will let him.

"Just give me a chance. A *chance* is all."

\*\*\*

Across town, Rita and Louis are walking down the hallway in another playgroup. Louis looking at the numbers on the doors, says, "Here it is. This is Richard's." Without knocking, he opens the door and they both walk in on a brown fellow who is sitting on his bed, more of a cot, in his small cubicle. Their unannounced entrance startles him. He sits up straight and tries to conceal the marijuana joint he has been pulling on. His face reflects his surprise and concern as he does his best to maintain his cool. He tries to hide his illegal activity by putting it behind his back. The long ash drops off however and now he has to put out a little smoldering problem with the one free hand.

He has an embarrassed, shit grin on his face as he says, "Hey, man, Louis."

"Hi man," Louis greets him and sniffs the marijuana. "I mean, High, man." He laughs.

"Say, how *do* you manage to get that stuff? You *always* score. I never knew how, but I knew you'd have the stash."

Richard looks at Rita and in a high falsetto says, "Score? What you talkin' 'bout, LOU-IS-SS?" His body language is; *What the f, man! You're here with a female.*

*I can get burnt for blowing stuff and here you are talking about it. Dumb, Louis. Not cool, Louis. Not cool at all, Louis.* Then out loud, "What are you talking about, brother? Huh, Louis, ol' buddy?"

Louis laughs. Rita picks up the joint that Richard had nonchalantly dropped on the floor and she relights it. She takes a big hit then passes it back to Richard. He ignores her, refusing to touch the joint. She spits out a loose leaf and says, "Umm, good smoke, Richard."

Richard just smiles, a huge shit-grin smile at her. He is still not too sure about all this. In fact, he is stoned and not really prepared to handle this sudden drama. He does his best to maintain as he tries to figure out how to extradite himself.

Louis pats him on the shoulder. "Let me introduce my girlfriend, Rita. Rita this is Richard."

"Hi, Richard," Rita gives him a hug. "I've heard so much about you from Louis."

"You have?"

"Yes, of course. He considers you one of his best friends. Told me all about some of the adventures you two have been through together."

"He has?" Richard still worried about getting busted looks over to Louis who has taken the joint that Rita had held out to Richard but which he refused to take.

"Absolutely," Louis says from behind a wall of smoke that he exhales.

"How wonderful," Richard says in his falsetto, meaning the opposite.

Rita smiles at Richard and explains, "Louis and I have been close friends for months."

Richard, still nervous and trying to cope with his high and the possible trouble at hand, "Close friends?"

"Very close," Rita says.

"Very, close," Louis nods agreement.

"Very close," Rita repeats, "in fact we've been living together for two months and having a great time."

"Living together?" Richard asks.

"Living to-geth-*ther*," Louis half sings it.

"They got playgroups where females live wit-ja? What playgroup is that? What's the name of it?"

"No, not in a playgroup, Richard," Rita explains. "We've been together on the outside."

"The outside?" Richard asks. He considers, then grins, like he gets it, it's a joke. "Okay, I get it now."

"No, really," Rita says.

"Yes, sir," Louis adds. "I've been living with Rita at her place." He takes another hit off of the joint.

Richard watches him, tries to sort it all out in his head.

"We've come to get you out," Rita says. "What do you think? Want to try it?"

"Well I..." Richard is interrupted by Louis' coughing spasm.

Louis is blinded by the smoke. He has tears in his eyes and is coughing. With his eyes closed he hands the joint back to Rita but this time, Richard reaches out and takes it. Richard has a long pull, holds it, and releases it slowly, all the time watching for Rita's reaction.

She has none.

Louis finally gets his words out, "Show him the papers, Rita. Richard, look, check it out."

Rita presses her watch and their authorization papers appear in a three-dimensional image that pops out into the air between them. She grabs it, expands it and hands it to Richard. He reads the image slowly, hindered by his marijuana high.

"This part right here," Rita points to the relevant paragraph. "You see? Your name and orders for you to be released into our custody."

Richard looks up at her with a shit-grin. "Really? No-shit?"

"Yeah, Rich. You're getting out," Louis says.

Rita smiles at him. Richard laughs. Louis laughs, then the two of them are over powered by the marijuana and suffer from a serious case of the giggles. Rita tries to bring them back so they can move on.

"If you two would calm down, we could move this along," She says, smiling from one to the other.

Richard stops laughing. "You're right. Show me the way."

"What do you want to take with you," she asks.

"Hmm, good question." Richard gets up and opens his closet. He begins to lay shirts and pants and robes out on his cot. He stops and turns to them and asks them, "Say, you're not kidding me, are you? This isn't some Femeronian psychological test, is it?"

Louis, feeling his friend's fear says seriously, "No, Rich. It's true. Honest. You're getting out. This is your freedom, man."

Rita goes over and hugs Richard. "I know you're worried but look, even if we *are* wrong, which we're not, the worst thing that could happen is they bring you back here."

"No," Richard shakes his head, "the worse thing that could happen is they lock me up in Max Security instead of bringing me back here."

Rita and Louis look at him. They realize he's right. There could be bad consequences for these males if the Femeron leaders want to make an example out of them.

***

Dr. Joy and Milon walk along a wide walkway towards a low, single story cement building. Above the double glass entrance doors, a large white sign reads, BUILDING C-J MAXIMUM SECURITY. And in smaller letters underneath, Authorized Personnel Only.

Dr. Joy buzzes the door. A female's guard's face appears in a 3-D image outside the glass doors. "State your business," the image says in a robotic voice. The image has moved right up to Dr. Joy. She takes a step back from it and speaks to it as if it were a person.

"We have authorization to meet with several of your inmates."

"Show said authorization."

Dr. Joy downloads the authorization document from her watch and takes the 3-D hologram image and holds it up to the guard's face. "Said authorization," she says with a touch of attitude.

"And the male?"

"He's to help me with the interrogation."

"Advance," the robotic voice and image fade and the double glass doors slide open.

Dr. Joy looks at Milon, they both take a breath and walk in. Before then can continue down the hall, they must pass through two sensor booths. Images of them appear in hologram form. The computer turns each image around to display every angle. All of their body parts and the objects in their pockets are shown in detail. Images of Dr. Joy's several devices are blown up in separate images. Alongside each image are numbers representing measurements and energy potentials.

Once cleared by the sensors, Dr. Joy and Milon are led down a long hallway by another floating image of a female guard. They walk past monitoring stations and through locked doors into another long hallway. There is no artwork on the walls as in the other playgroups. The furnishings, what there are of them, are industrial. The atmosphere is cold and impersonal.

When they arrive at a monitoring station, real female guards stop them.

"May I see your authorization again?" The female guard sitting at the security station says. Her voice is a bit metallic and her eyes seem to stare rather than focus.

Dr. Joy turns to Milon. "They're robots. Quite well done. Don't you think?"

"Amazing," Milon agrees.

"Your papers, please," the guard says. "And we are humanoids, not *robots*."

"I beg your pardon," Dr. Joy apologizes as she presents the 3-D image of the authorization papers.

The female guard expands the image and reads it carefully. She looks up at Milon, then over to Dr. Joy.

"You are here to interview male inmates, Paul and Max. Is that correct?" She says, and once again looks suspiciously at Milon.

"Yes, that's correct," Dr. Joy confirms.

"We can bring them both out to the conference room next to the day room, just down the hall, here," she motions with her head.

"Actually, I would like to speak with them outside. If you don't mind."

"Outside?"

"Yes, in the yard, please." Joy smiles.

The guard does not smile back. "In the yard? No, I don't think that will be possible."

"Actually," Dr. Joy becomes serious, "you will note that my authorization papers states that I am to meet with them in private."

"The conference room, is *private*," the guard is a bit sarcastic.

"Sure it is," Rita doesn't back down. "Are you going to honor the authorization order or not?"

The guard does not answer, but reads through the document again.

"If I have to, I will contact the capital city leadership," Joy points to the guard. "They will contact the warden of Max Security, who will contact your boss who, I'm pretty certain will not appreciate the call down. And I assume they will let you know about it. Perhaps they will require a maintenance check of your software for a logic malfunction."

The female guard looks at her, not convinced. Rita shrugs. "It will mean a lot of paperwork for your bosses and the leadership, but hey, I'm sure they won't mind the extra work, right?"

The guard makes eye contact. "All right, you may meet with them in the yard, but why does this male need to meet with them?" She looks Milon up and down and then back to Dr. Joy.

"We have official business with the inmates. I am not free to discuss that work with you."

"I see," the guard nods. "Some type of investigation? Well, I wouldn't doubt it with these two. Paul and Max are bright ones all right. Almost too smart for their own good."

"Whatever," Rita waves the question off with the back of her hand.

The guard hesitates, shakes her head and says, "Alright. I will have someone show you out to the yard. Paul and Max will meet you there."

"Thank you," Dr. Joy says. "And one more thing more," she makes eye contact with the guard, "if they are wearing wires, I will end the interview and contact my people. Like I said before, lots of paperwork and not so happy bosses."

The female guard nods. She buzzes and another female guard, also in a grey uniform comes up to the guard station.

"Follow me," the second guard says.

"Is this one a humanoid too or flesh and blood?" Milon asks as the guard leads them down the hallway.

"I think she's an H." Dr. Joy shrugs.

"Pretty impressive," Milon says. "I wonder, do they like to bang too?"

"You would wonder that," Dr. Joy says.

Through a security door and outside, Dr. Joy and Milon wait on a grass field for a half an hour before the door opens again and two inmates are led out. The guard walks behind them, motioning them to join Dr. Joy and Milon.

When they arrive, Dr. Joy nods to the guard, "That will be all," she says, and in case the guard had any thoughts of staying with them, she points toward the door.

The guard leaves and the two inmates, Dr. Joy and Milon, all watch as she reaches the door and goes back inside. Still there is tension in the air. Milon reaches out and shakes hands with both of the males.

"Dr. Joy, this is Paul, Paul – Dr. Joy." They do not shake.

"And this is Max." Max also makes no effort to shake her hand.

"Milon has told me good things about you both," Dr. Joy tries to make conversation. Both Paul and Max stare at her, devoid of facial expressions.

Paul is the taller of the two. He has blond hair cut long and uncombed. He is slimmer than Max too. His blue eyes are intense. He is observing and calculating. Max is a few inches shorter with black hair and dark features. He is not smiling, but he doesn't seem as intense as Paul. They both look defiant as they exude toughness. They show complete disdain for the female but do seem at ease with Milon.

"Milon has told me some stories of you three growing up together," Dr. Joy continues. "You've known each other a long time. Am I right?"

As before, neither male responds or changes expressions.

"Some of those days were difficult times and experiences," she continues but when they still do not respond she shrugs. "Well, okay then. Before we begin, Milon has to do a quick search. "Milon, please," she nods toward the two prisoners and Milon takes out a small device.

"Just precautions for your safety and ours," he says as he shows them the device. "May I?"

They both nod approval and he slides it first up and down Paul, then over Max's body. There is no beeping alert so he places the detector back in his pocket.

"You realize of course that they have listening devices?" Max asks Milon.

"Yes," Dr. Joy responds. "Not a problem. Milon, if you will."

Milon nods agreement to her request and takes out yet another device. When he switches it on, a humming noise is emitted.

"This will block them," she says. "Our conversations are now off the record." She pauses, looks from one to the other.

"We need to turn our backs to them," Paul says.

"Turn our backs?" Dr. Joy asks.

"They can zoom in and read our lips."

"I see. Okay then, let's all turn our backs to the building," They all turn away from the building.

"You are probably wondering," Milon tries to move the conversation along for her, "why I would bring you to an interview with a female with some authority?"

"As a matter of fact, yes Milon. What's up?" Paul looks first to Milon and then to Dr. Joy. Max follows the discussion without responding.

"Dr. Joy has taken me out of my playgroup and brought me to her home outside the city where I live free."

Max looks incredulous.

"She has a plan to free more men and I have recommended you two."

"Really? And what's the catch?" Paul asks.

"No catch," Milon says. "It's just that…"

"Actually, there is a catch," Dr. Joy interjects. "If you want to call it that."

"And what's that?" Max asks.

"You have to answer questions before a panel of Femeron leaders."

"Well that's a catch all right," Paul laughs at her.

"Is that before or after they cut our balls off?" Max adds.

"Oh, well-well after," Dr. Joy says with a wave of her hand.

Milon laughs. Dr. Joy smiles. Paul and Max eventually break into grins.

"And how do you plan to do this? Walk us out the front door?" Paul asks.

"I wish we had that option," Dr. Joy says, "but I don't believe they are going to allow us do that and it might take weeks of discussions. We don't have that kind of time. No, I've made other plans."

"So how do you propose pulling this great escape off?" Paul asks. "You do realize that these guards are authorized to kill, right?"

Max interjects. "Yes, that's right, Paul said, 'Kill' and believe me, man, would they ever like the chance to rub us out."

"I understand there are some risks involved," Dr. Joy says.

"Some risks? Shit, lady," Paul speaks using his hands for emphasis. "You're gonna have to understand, I haven't been exactly the model citizen in here. These females have a right to hold a grudge against me."

"I'm not their favorite either," Max puts in.

"If we give them a chance to use their lasers on us, they will." Paul makes a gesture with his hand to indicate a hand gun.

"Tell her like it is, Paul," Max encourages him. "Tell'em, you know, what's come down around here in the last six months. Shit, Milon, do you realize you are risking *your* life to try and bust us out?"

"Yes," Milon responds. "We've spent time going over the different scenarios with…"

"Different scenarios?" Paul almost growls. "C'mon, man. This isn't some game show. These females are seriously crazy! Do I have to remind you that lasers cut right through skin and bone?"

"No, I get it but…"

"You are not going to be shot," Joy interrupts Milon. "I will guarantee you that much. The worst that can happen is after you testify before the Femeron council, is that they would send you back here."

"Yeah, right," Paul says.

"*And*, I have many important friends that would do all they can to make life easier for you. Perhaps get you out of Max Security. And that's if we fail. If we succeed, your lives will change a lot and all for the better."

"I don't know," Max shakes his head.

"And, not just for you but for thousands of other males as well," Dr. Joy adds.

"One thing, lady," Paul says in a low voice filled with anger. "I get the chance to get outside and you're stuck inside with these guards, don't count on me to help you. No, and don't hold us back when it's time to run for it."

Dr. Joy turns to Milon and says, "I'm not so sure I agree with your selection of males." Turning towards Paul and Max and pointing with her thumb, "If this is your example of an advanced male, there's serious doubts about your mental processes, Honey. Because this guy is a prime candidate for Monkey of the Month award."

Milon laughs. He winks at her. "Trust me on this one, Joy. These guys are born actors. Paul has been playing with you. He's got a million personalities and he works them all to mess over people's minds." Milon waves his wrist, palms down. "I've seen them in action and I'm one of the few who knows their real selves."

He turns and looks Paul in the face, "Right, Diego?"

"Yeah, right, Mike," Paul nods.
Dr. Joy looks confused.
"Childhood nicknames," Milon explains.
"And Max?" she asks.
"Just plain ol' Max," Max says.
"Listen, we aren't getting anywhere standing here diagnosing my fractured personality," Paul says.
"Agreed," Dr. Joy says.
"So how do you plan to pull this off?" Dr. Joyfull?
"Come on, Paul," Milon says. "This is no time for confrontations. She's trying to help you."
"Oh yeah?" Paul stares at Dr. Joy.
"I think I agree with brother, Mike on this, Paul," Max says. "Let's hear her out."
"Okay," Paul nods. "Sorry about that. Old habits die hard."
"Apology accepted," Joy looks first to Paul then to Max. "What we plan is to transport you out of here using the Laser Particle Transporter system," she looks at each of them again. "Are you familiar with this technology?"
"Heard of it," Max says.
"Read about it," Paul concurs.
"It is perfectly safe," Joy continues. "When we get to the Laser Transport room, you are going to step into a laser light."
"Step into it?" Max asks.
"Yes," she nods. "It's quite easy. Just walk into the light. Before you know it, you will step out in a Laser

Particle Receiver room in the capital. From there, my people will take care of everything. Housing, food, security, everything up to the day you are to testify before the Femeron leadership council."

"I don't know about this," Max says.

"Yeah, we could get shredded," Paul adds.

"I've done it a number of times," Milon says, "and there were never any problems."

"No problems?" Paul repeats.

"That's right, no problems and no after affects.
"Perfectly safe," Milon says, trying to convince them.

"It is perfectly safe," Dr. Joy reiterates, "as long as you step completely into the laser light. Don't holdback and half step in."

"No half steppin'?" Paul smiles.

"No," Dr. Joy says seriously. "No half-stepping."

Neither Paul or Max seem convinced. Milon adds,

"I will go in first." He looks at each of them. "So just follow me in."

"As quickly as you can," Dr. Joy adds. "The guards may try to stop you, so go right after Milon."

"And no half-steppin'," Max won't leave it alone.

Dr. Joy nods, then turns to Paul. "Well? What do you think?"

"I think what you're trying to pull off here is very dangerous," he says. "And despite your guarantees, things could go really bad, really quick."

Joy does not respond and Paul continues. "I'm not doing this recklessly. You understand? We need to be smart. We need to know exactly what we're doing. Can you assure me of this? That you've put in the time and done all that can be done to have a successful outcome?"

"Yes," Dr. Joy nods. "I can assure you that we've studied this and worked out the details over and over. Nobody wants this to be successful more than I do."

Neither respond. "I'm glad too that you have voiced your concern," she goes on. "I'm confident that this is far from reckless."

"Okay, well let's do it then. Right, Max?" Paul turns to his friend.

"Yeah, it's a go for me too," Max agrees.

"Great," Dr. Joy says. "Milon, cover me while I speak to R."

"Will do," Milon walks over to Dr. Joy and stands with his back touching hers. He activates his handheld device and microwaves encircle them, blocking any eaves dropping.

Dr. Joy speaks into her diamond pin on her blouse. "'R'? This is it. Do you have us?" She listens to Rita's response then turns to the group. "We need to get to the Laser Transport Room," Dr. Joy says. "From what I saw on the blueprints of the building, it's on the second floor at the back of the building and it looks like the only way there is past the main guard station."

"Well that's going to be a fun moment or two," Milon says.

"Actually," Max says, "I know how to get there using the utility elevator."

"Can you get us through the building to that elevator?" Milon asks.

"I'm gonna try," Max nods.

"Alright, this is it. Let me do the talking but be ready if I need you to get physical." Joy looks at each of the men, then begins to walk toward the building.

With tense faces, the four walk across the field and to the door where the guard is waiting to let them back in.

"I need to go to your Laser Transporter room," Joy tells the guard.

"What, with these two?" The guard nods towards Paul and Max.

"Yes, that's right." Joy says. "I'm from the Genetic Scientific Council. I've been sent here to bring these males to a testing laboratory. And, I'm on a tight schedule, so if you would please…"

"Yeah, no, you're not going anywhere with these two," the guard stands her ground blocking the doorway.

"Please, you're obstructing my mission." Joy goes to shoulder the guard out of the way.

"No, doctor," she says as she pulls her laser gun from her belt.

Dr. Joy stops dead in her tracks. "Now hold on a minute," Dr. Joy takes two steps back. "You don't want to make a huge mistake here. I have authorization from the Femeron Council to take these males with me."

"I need to see those written instructions," the guard says without lowering her laser gun.

"Certainly, you don't think I came all this way without the proper documents?"

The guard just nods for her to get her the papers. Dr. Joy inputs onto her watch's screen and a hologram image appears, her authorization form. "Look here, signed by the Regional Femeron representative." Dr. Joy moves the floating image for the guard to handle it. The guard reads the 3-D image and shakes her head.

"Yeah, no. This doesn't fly. Sorry but three signatures

are required in order to remove inmates. That's code section 1245 A-three..."

"Oh, please," Dr. Joy says, annoyed. "You can't overrule a councilor's orders!"

"I know this one," Paul says. "She is as dumb as she looks." He points to the image that the guard is still holding. "I sure hope headquarters hears about this fiasco."

"Oh, they are going to all right," Dr. Joys raises her voice. "Let me have my image back," she reaches out for the document and as the guard returns it, Dr. Joy grabs the wrist of the hand holding the laser pistol and hits her with an elbow to the jaw. The guard is knocked down and out. The laser gun falls to the floor inside the hallway. Max picks it up.

"No, Max," Joy explains. "If we're armed, they have the right to shoot us." She nods toward the gun in his hand. "Hide it so this one can't find it when she wakes."

Max throws the laser gun into a trash can.

"We better get out of Dodge," Milon says.

"Great movie, by the way," Paul adds.

"Loved it, especially the part where they make their escape," Dr. Joy says.

"Okay, this way to the utility elevator," Max takes off jogging down the hall, then a sharp left at the first intersection of hallways.

The guard has recovered her senses and sits up. She watches the four running away and looks around for her laser gun but can't locate it. She gets up and opens a control panel on the wall and inputs her codes. In front of Dr. Joy and the men, a metal partition comes slowly sliding out of the wall, once it is all the way across, it will seal off the hallway. The males make it past the moving steel barricade. Dr. Joy running to catch up has very little chance of making it in time. The males stand aghast as the thick, steel door grinds ever closer to shutting her out. To speed up, she dives head first and slides along the marble floor and past the barricade. With the barest of margins, she has made it to them and lies at their feet and looks up and smiles. The barricade has sealed off the hallway behind them and for the moment they are safe from the guard.

"You know, Joy," Paul says as he reaches down to help her to her feet. "I'm starting to like you more and more."

"That's Doctor Joy, if you don't mind," she says.

"Don't mind at all, *Doctor* Joy."

"Yeah, nice slide, honey," Milon adds. "Saw that in a movie too." She laughs.

"I hate to break up this 'All for One' meeting," Max says. "But, hey, c'mon, let's get out of here."

"He's right," Joy says as she brushes dust from her clothes. "We've got to find that transporter, quick."

As they jog down the hallway, the barricade partition behind them begins to re-open.

"I think she may be pissed off," Paul says.

"You've got her thing-a-ma-jig?" Milon asks.

"Her key, yeah." Joy holds up a small device.

"We can go through here," Max points to a door just before the end of the hallway.

"But the LPT's on the second floor," Dr. Joy objects. "Look, up this stairway." She points up a stairwell to their right.

"Sure," Max says, "but first we go outside, then back in through doors farther down. That way the guards will be searching for us here. And, we can open the outside doors as we pass them. We can let *everyone* out! Can you imagine? Everyone making a break for it at the same time."

"No, no, no," Dr. Joy interrupts him. "Not now, Max. That would complicate things. We'd have to explain too much to too many. It would really hurt our plans for the Femeron Summit Meeting."

"I told you man," Max has turned to Milon. "Chicken-shit. They're all Chicken-Shit."

"Hey," Milon yells back at him. "She didn't come her to free all you idiots. Just you two. Either do what she says or go it alone."

"Milon, this is a chance of a lifetime." Max argues. "Look what they've done to our lives. We have a chance to really mess with them."

"Then what?" Milon asks. "In two or three days, everyone is caught and back here with time added to their sentences. How does that help anyone?"

"Milon's right, and besides," Paul looks to Max, "it isn't like we have all day to discuss this."

"So, let's move it," Dr. Joy says and takes off up the stairway.

Taking two steps at a time, Max yells up to her from behind, "Okay, have it your way, but you're still Chicken-Shit, Lady!"

"The Whole World is Chicken-Shit, Sucker!" Milon yells out.

"Well, maybe everything except the blast from a laser gun," Paul yells. "That's no Chicken-Shit."

They have reached the top of the steep stairs and Joy is attempting to open the locked metal door. Paul sees a guard at the bottom of the stairs and yells out, "OOO Chicken-Shit!"

The stairwell door opens and they all rush inside just as the guard fires her laser gun. The vicious laser blast streaks through the air with a deadly, electronic whine. The first of the guard's two shots goes through the open door and over their heads. It hits the far wall of the hall upstairs and burns a hole in the metal that is gruesome to behold. The laser's heat actually melts the metal, then when it hardens again, it looks like melted wax. The second laser shot hits the closing door and burns a hole through it.

"Damn," Milon shouts.

"Looks like she doesn't have it on stun," Max points out.

"You think?" Joy agrees.

"Let's go!" She yells and runs down the hallway.

Max takes the lead. "This way," he points for them to make the first right.

"Looks like they are serious about keeping you boys here," Milon adds as Max passes him.

"I'll miss them too." Max jokes.

At the end of this hallway, Max stops at a door. "Okay, wait," Max pulls up. "On the other side of this door is the LPT room."

"Well, let's go. C'mon then," Milon says.

"Not so fast," Max says. "There's probably a squad of guards there to block us."

"And even if we get past the guards, they could have disabled the LPT," Paul warns.

"No, uh-uh," Dr. Joy says. "My people overrode the controls here, just in case we had trouble. She's got that thing humming, waiting for us to jump in."

"That was good planning, Joy," Paul says.

"That's Doctor Joy to you," Joy answers.

"Well, Doctor, how do we get to it if there are guards?" Max asks.

"I'll have to go in first. Check it out and..."

"And?" Max interrupts.

"And, well, I don't know. We'll just have to play it by ear."

Max rolls his eye balls.

"Just one thing, *doctor*," Paul says.

"What's that?"

"If they give us a chance to surrender, take it. Please."

"If they give us a chance to surrender," Max interrupts, "give'em the finger!"

"Oh Lord," Paul moans.

"Sounds like you don't want to leave your happy home here," Milon says.

"Oh, sure he does." Max puts his arm around Paul's shoulder. "It's just that he gets emotional when he thinks of blood."

"I never really wanted to do anything but keep on keeping on. This is getting pretty scary," Paul admits.

"Okay, okay," Dr. Joy interjects. "I'll leave the door open. Listen for my signal, and come running." She opens the door with her electronic key, and a large section of the wall begins to slide open. It is 10 centimeters of thick stainless steel yet it slides open noiselessly. The smoothness of the opening door seems to calm them as they peer into the next room.

Joy steps through the opened doorway into a large room with several hallways intersecting it. She leaves the door open behind her. The males stay out of sight, their backs against the wall.

Joy walks into the room as casual as she can make herself. She doesn't see anyone but she's suspicious that there are guards hiding. She gets closer to the LPT's opening and can hear it humming with energy, just as Rita had promised it would be. She walks to within six meters of the LPT.

"This is too easy," she says to herself. "Nobody here? And I'm standing around checking it out until, what? Until they arrive?"

She turns and yells at them, "C'mon, C'MON! Let's GO!"

The three males come running through the doorway. As they approach her, guards suddenly appear from around the corner at the far end of the room. Another door slides open and six more guards jog into the room. Paul, Max, Milon and Joy stop dead in their tracks. They look from the guards to the opening, humming with the laser lights of the LPT.

The guard leader, seeing their calculations advises them, "Don't even think about it." She points with her laser gun. "You can't outrun a laser, so don't make the mistake of trying."

"Just freeze," the guard walking up to them says. She and two others go behind them, another guard in front motions for them to start walking away from the LPT, toward the guard leader. When they have gone 5 steps, Paul jumps on the leading guard's back.

"Yiiiii!!" he screams as she falls forward from the surprise weight.

Max quickly rips her laser gun out of her hand and holds it to her head as she lays underneath Paul.

Max looks up to the guards and smiles. "Now *you* freeze!" he says it with authority.

The guard leader holds her hand up to signal the other guards to obey.

"Okay, now Gent-tel-lee put'em down on the floor," Max keeps his eye contact with the females.

No one moves. Max's face is very serious, "Okay, want to play it out? I'm betting it goes down like this: I will shoot her brains out, then still have time to get two or three of you before I'm hit. Want to play with me, girls?"

"Max," Milon says. "No need to get them mad."

"Oh, I think there is," Max responds with an evil look. He looks into each of the guards' faces. "This will be pay back for all the times they've insulted and disrespected me."

"Bottom line," Dr. Joy says to the guard leader, "is you have chosen to interfere with a fully authorized mission of the Femeron Scientific Council. I have shown you people their authorization, but you have chosen to interfere and have even fired deadly shots at us. I predict this will end very badly for all of you."

The guard leader stares at Dr. Joy while she considers her options.

"Better to let us go, no one gets hurt and you can file all the complaints and charges you feel are required." Joy nods to her.

"Lay'em down," Max reiterates.

"Okay, but relax," the guard leader says. "We're going to put our lasers down. Don't get tense. You relax first so you don't start killing…"

"Hey!" Max screams at her. "Just do it! Lay'em down and no I am not going to relax. If you are thinking of playing games with me, this place is going to turn into one hell-of-a-light show."

"All right," the leader says, then to the other guards. "Let's do as he wants and nobody, I repeat, nobody acts on their own."

Max watches as they deposit their firearms on the tile floor. "Okay, nice and slow and gently, *Girls*."

"Oh, Christ, Max," Milon says. "Would you quit being an ass so we can get out of here?"

The guards, however insulted and angry they may be, do place their guns on the floor and stand back. Paul gets up off of the guard he has been laying on. His movement breaks the spell over Milon and Joy as they and Paul have all been absolutely motionless since the moment Max yelled, "Freeze!" But now that they have the upper hand, they come to life.

"Man, you are crazy, Max," Joy says with a sigh of relief.

"But you're getting to like me though, right?" Max smiles.

"Yeah, sure, you are now an all-time favorite of mine," Joy can't help but smile back.

'Okay, please no marriage proposals," Max says, holding up his hands in mock protest. "I've had a long and trying day."

"And it isn't over yet," Paul adds.

"And it isn't over yet," Max nods in agreement.

They step closer to the LPT. Max keeps his laser pointed at the guards. He is walking backwards and as Milon, Paul and Joy reach the LPT's entrance and stop, Max backs into them by accident. This slight collision adds enough pressure to Max's grip on the laser gun's trigger that it causes him to fire a shot. This wild shot fires a burst of white-hot light. It hits the wall across from the LPT with a SLAM and instantly melts a good chunk of the solid steel wall. The sudden blast so surprises Max that it knocks the laser gun out of his hand and as it falls to the floor, everyone stands and looks at it in shock.

The guards had instinctively ducked their heads when the shot was fired. Milon, Paul and Joy had turned halfway around, frightened by the sound of the laser's blast and now, for an instant, everyone is in a sort of limbo. This quiet atmosphere, with just the sound of the wall sizzling where the laser beam has melted it, and the humming of the LPT is quickly broken by Max's voice as he yells out, "OOOOOOOOH SHIT!" He is moving quick as he can to the LPT. He bumps his friends as he rushes past them towards the entrance.

The guards meanwhile, also awakened by Max's scream, go for their guns. Before they can pick up their lasers, the four have jumped into the LPT's magic light and have vanished. Without hesitating, the captain of the guards picks up her laser gun and runs to the Laser Particle Transporter's. With five of the guards behind her, she runs into the LPT's light in hot pursuit of the escapees.

Outside the high security building, two quick bursts of intense light shoot out of its tower and streak toward the capital.

\*\*\*

In the main control room of the LPT system, Rita and Louis sit in front of the large, wall screen where the two flashes of laser lights are being tracked.

"Uh oh," Rita says.

"What, uh oh?" Louis asks. "What's the matter?"

"It looks like Dr. Joy has made more friends then she cared to," Rita points to the second red dot, trailing the first.

"What can you do?"

"First thing to do is to place them both into holding patterns." She focuses on the control panel board and inputs instructions in a complicated maneuver of computer inputting. Rita's hands are fluid and fast. Outside the office windows, the two beams flash by overhead. The speed and energy of the two broad beams is seen, heard and felt as they go by at fantastic speed. The sound they make is a loud, powerful rumble which quickly fades as the sections of light whizz off into the distance.

On the screen, the two red flashing beams begin to circle the city. Rita and Louis watch the indicator as it tracks the red dots. Rita is calculating on her hologram hand calculator. She is looking back and forth from the tracking screen to the image hanging in mid-air before her. She continues to enter minor adjustments into the controls.

"Now what?" Louis asks as he watches her work.

"Well, it's tricky," she says without looking up.

"How's that?" he asks looking over her shoulder.

"We had the beam at full power so we could get them out of there fast. But now there's two groups on the beam and if we land them anywhere, they're so close together they'd all smash full force into the receivers."

"And into each other," Louis adds.

"That's right, and into each other, which would be messy."

"Well, slow them down then," Louis says, thinking that he's found the simple answer.

Rita, still continuing the math calculations. "I don't, think I can." she says. This time she looks up at him. "If we did, there's a chance that the second group would catch up to the front one and they'd be one crazy looking body when they finally did land."

"Oh boy," Louis scratches his head.

"Exactly." she pauses then adds, "Actually it's quite an interesting problem in laser particle transporting. The physics involved is really very challenging."

"Yeah, right," he says cynically, "I'm sure you'll rewrite the textbooks after this one."

"Just might," Rita responds quietly as she concentrates on her calculations. "Un-hmm, just might."

"You come up with something?" Louis watches as she continues to calculate.

"Yes. Maybe. It hasn't been tried before but it's possible. I think it should work."

Rita goes from her hologram calculator floating in the air to one of the large accessory computers near the console's tracking board. She only has to reach up and another hologram calculator keypad appears where ever she places her fingers. Her input brings an immediate response from the computer and Rita checks the resultant numbers. This new info brings an optimistic, bright tone to her voice.

"Umm-hmm. Just might. Yeah, I think this should work."

Louis is watching her moves and facial expressions closely. "Should?"

"Well, could."

"But should is better than could, right?" he asks.

"Whatever," Rita says concentrating on the numbers.

Rita, still reading from the computer and inputting more formulas. "Okay, go over to that standing console there." She points to the mainframe built into the wall.

Louis walks over to the mainframe, "Now what?"

Rita looks back at her computer screen. "We're going to try to direct the first carrying segment to its planned destination here, then cut the beam behind them and re-direct the second segment back to the receiver unit at the Maximum-Security building."

"Send them home, heh?"

"Yes, if we can," Rita says. "Look up at the tracking board and I'll show you."

The tracking board's black screen fills half a wall above the mainframe. On it, blinking lights track the two LPT laser beams. "Now this is Joy's group," she points to the first blinking red light as it moves across the screen. "And this one's her unwanted admirers."

"I got that already," Louis says.

"Yes, of course. Okay, then, when the first blinking light comes to this exact spot," she points to the spot on the black screen. "I will input my change and re-direct it here, to our receiving unit."

"Okay, good."

"But a moment later the other red dot will reach that same location, before it does, you need to press this control button to send it on a route back to the maximum receiver."

"Got it. Wait, which button?" Louis is looking at his hologram keyboard floating in the room by his hand.

"Just hit, control-enter," Rita advises.

"Okay that I can do."

"You have to enter that just one blink before they come to this spot." She points again to the screen location.

"It's going to be tight," Louis shakes his head.

"That's why I need your help. It's all in the timing."

"What isn't?"

"True," Rita agrees.

She and Louis watch the red lights on the tracking board. It shows the two LPT laser beams as they head around the city on another round of their circular holding pattern. The lights approach the spot where Rita will redirect the first beam.

"Okay, you ready?"

"Yeah," Louis says in a weak voice.

"Better let them have one more go around," Rita says and outside the two beams zoom past overhead as citizens look up and point to them.

She and Louis are focused on the red lights on the large screen as the two beams make another circuit over the city.

"Okay, here they come again," Rita tenses.

The red blinking lights click closer and closer to the planned point of action. Both Rita and Louis wait in heightened anticipation.

When the first blinking light comes to the exact spot Rita has calculated, she inputs onto her keyboard. The first red light makes a turn on the screen. A loud, bright laser beam passes through the Laser Beam Receiver in the next room and we see Dr. Joy, Milon, Paul and Max tumble out. They are propelled out of the LPT and the force behind their landing knocks them immediately off balance. This violent arrival throws them across the smooth floor and they land in a pile of arms, legs and asses. All intertwined together, sprawled out at the far corner of the room. Meanwhile, Louis distracted by their sudden arrival, and only very late, turns back to the screen and sees the second blinking red light.

"LOUIS!" Rita shouts.

"OH-Shit!" he responds and hits the two buttons on his keyboard.

"We made it!" Paul says from the floor.

Dr. Joy, looking around, "I don't think we're fused together."

"Best friggin' ride I've ever been on," Max laughs.

"Really," Milon agrees.

"They need to work on that landing part just a little," Paul adds. He feels his arms and shoulders for broken bones.

Rita turns back to the screen and watches as the second blinking red light flies off the screen and into the unknown.

"Where are they headed?" Louis asks.

"Lord, knows," Rita responds. She concentrates on her computer readings and says, "Looks like you've sent them to the Laser Receiver Unit on Guam."

"On *Guam*?"

"Yes. They're on track to be received at the Rod Rosenstein/Bruce Ohr Corrupt Officials Holding Facility."

"Oh, Lordy, Lordy," Louis moans.

# Chapter Eight
## What This is All About

Dr. Joy and her two assistants walk up the many marble stepped entrance of the General Assembly building in Femeron City. They pass security checkpoints then go through the crowded marble lobby to the doors at the rear of the assembly auditorium. As they open the door, loud rock music pounds over the public address system. They stand just inside the doors and look around. The auditorium is shaped like an amphitheater. The work stations in the back of the large assembly hall are elevated so that each region's representatives have unobstructed views of the stage. Lolan spots Counselor Paula sitting at her console half way down the aisle. She points to her and the three women walk down the carpeted aisle.

In front of the assembly hall there is a raised stage. On stage is a long table for the assembly's procedures committee and behind the committee, on the back wall of the room, there is a very large video screen. To the left of the head table is the speaker's platform and podium.

The meeting is already in progress. The rock music that played during the break, stops as Dr. Joy and her colleagues join Paula and her people. They greet each other with tense but smiling faces. They know that in a matter of minutes Paula will take the speaker's stand.

"The Genetics committee has presented their explanations of the Triple X cloning crisis," Paula brings Dr. Joy up to speed. "They have offered three recommendations for possible actions to be taken to find the causes. I'm going to offer our recommendation before a vote is taken."

Dr. Joy nods her head in approval and Paula brings up the Chairperson's image on her console's screen. The chairperson recognizes Paula.

"Paula, have you been briefed on the cloning crisis and issues?"

"I have, yes. We've considered it at length and I wish to address the assembly on a possible alternative solution. One not brought forth by the Genetics Committee."

"Alright," the female chairperson, a middle-aged woman says. "I will schedule you next."

"Very good, thank you." Paula exits the screen and refers to her notes.

"Well here goes," she says as she stands and walks off toward the raised speaker's podium. Dr. Joy and one of her aides walks by her side. As she approaches the dais, the chairperson announces her to the assembly.

"The Chair recognizes Region Five's Femeron representative, Paula Twenty."

"Thank you, thank you," Paula acknowledges the spattering of applause. "I would like to thank the Genetics Committee for their detailed analysis of the Triple X crisis and the dangers we face." Another smattering of applause.

"I take pride in the fact that ours is a civilization which faces crisis head on," Paula looks out over the packed assembly. "We have always solved the problems confronting us with a vigorous and sometimes non-conformist plan of action."

She pauses to look at individuals in the audience.

"We pride ourselves on our ability to think outside the box. Is that not one of our strengths as Femeron leaders? Of course it is and I think the present Triple X crisis deserves the same approach."

She pauses to look at the hologram copy of her speaking points floating above the podium in front of her.

"Our most competent cloning scientists tell us that the Triple X crises is accelerating at a rate that could very well require the complete shutdown of our breeding programs. In the meantime, each day, there are being created thousands of hopelessly deformed fetuses. Sadly, these fetuses must be destroyed and never allowed to mature."

She continues with an accentuation in her voice. "Think of it. Every day, thousands of live cultures must be destroyed because Triple X genes are being observed within the cells of these would-be children." She continues in a calmer voice. "Now, we have heard the presentation from the Genetics council. We have studied their recommendations and we acknowledge that they have submitted logical plans to provide research into the problem. But they do not, I repeat, they do *not* in any way address a solution to the problem right now. Right *now*, as this crisis grows each day." She raps the podium with her index finger. "Before our eyes we are watching the destruction of our young and they only want to *research* it?" She leans forward as she says this and makes eye contact with her fellow elected officials.

There is a titter among the audience. Paula continues in a raised voice.

"Yet *NONE* of them will guarantee success! Nor do any of them risk giving an estimate of the time needed to solve this dilemma." She looks around the hall, shaking her head in annoyance, even anger. "I say that we must," Paula taps the podium even harder with her index finger, "we *must* put into action a plan that will address the problem *immediately*."

The assembly breaks out into loud applause. The chairperson calls for silence.

Paula, feeding off the applause of approval, continues with confidence.

"The solution I am referring to comes from one of Femeron's most outstanding authorities. In the field of cloning science, there are few who have the theoretical or field experience as does, Dr. Joy." Paula is interrupted by heavy vocal rumblings. Undaunted, she continues. "I now present to this Summit," she has to shout to be heard over the uproar and the chairperson's gavel pounding and calls for order. "The distinguished Doctor of Cloning Science, Dr. Joy Fourteen." With these last few words, Paula steps aside and Dr. Joy joins her at the front of the podium. They touch cheeks and force a smile. Turning together to face the assembly they look out over an auditorium in the middle of loud and many voiced discussions.

"Just jump right in," Paula advises Dr. Joy. "They will stop, eventually."

Dr. Joy steps forward and in a clear, but nervous voice begins, "To the point, there is..." she is interrupted by the Chairperson's increased, sustained pounding and calls to order. When the assembly quiets, Dr. Joy goes on.

"There is one solution, scientifically infallible, that would end the Triple X gene phenomenon. Quite simply, we should stop using female cells in the fertilization process. We could easily substitute male sperm and never..."

Joy is immediately hard-put to overcome the uproar now emanating from the floor of the assembly. She tries, "And never have to fear...have to fear for the safety of the developing..." She must stop. She looks to the dais where the Chair, noting the energy of the turmoil, has decided to allow the commotion to continue before attempting to regain control.

The protests seem to be centered around three of the consoles located in the middle front section of the assembly hall. The chairperson recognizes the leader of that section. She is an older female and her manner is quite different from the others. She comes off as being angry and intolerant.

"The chair recognizes the representative from Region six, Dr. Meangala."

The older leader, already standing, shouts to be heard over the turmoil. She is exasperated and her mood is magnified by her purposely disheveled appearance. Her hair is frizzed out and brushed to look uncombed. Her make up is applied to look sloppy almost to the point of being grotesque.

"This is TOTALLY preposterous, AND out of order!"

Loud boos and jeers greet her.

"It is *insane* to suggest the *complete* contamination of our future generations." She tries to gather herself and continues in a more professional manner. "What Dr. Joy suggests we rightly deplore! The reintroduction of the male genes? Outrageous to eventhink it!"

More catcalls and boos. "Basic scientific knowledge and history, that's what Dr. Joy should be studying. Let's not forget the dangerous anti-social characteristics which males have always displayed."

Representative Meangala, struts back and forth, enjoying being the center of attention. She soaks in the cheers and scowls at the boos.

"That history is clear testimony to the males' influence on our human race..."

"Do you suggest that there has been no evolutionary advancement of the male?" Dr. Joy interrupts her from the speaker's podium. She in turn is then interrupted by shouts of protest but continues. "Of our species in the past 100 years?"

"Do *you* suggest there has been?" Meangala laughs and looks to her staff for support.

"I don't suggest it," Dr. Joy yells, "I state it as a *fact*!"

The laughter and turmoil reach a crescendo and subside.

"In this one region alone," Dr. Joy continues, "we have a hundred or more males that have evolved. Males that are worthy of breeding."

Representative Meangala's expression turns from laughter to anger.

"They have spent their lives in playgroups," Dr. Joy goes on, "and despite that stifling environment," she taps the back of one hand on the palm of her other hand to emphasize each word, "*despite being imprisoned since birth* by the Femeron government, they have advanced both emotionally and psychologically. They are in fact equals in every way to the females of our society."

Her last words are covered over by a loud cacophony of discussions.

The chairperson once again calls for order.

Dr. Joy looks directly at Representative Meangala and says, "May I present to you eighty-seven of these Free-Soul males for your education and enlightenment." Dr. Joy points to the doors on both sides of the auditorium. Attendants open the doors and males enter into the summit hall. They line up along the side walls amid cheers and boos. The males as they first enter the hall are silent, but then as they reach their places, they begin to talk amongst themselves and to the females nearby. It isn't long before they are laughing and loose.

The chairperson tries again to regain order. Her first attempts are fruitless and she stops and begins to converse instead with her fellow officials at the head table. Then, shaking her head in disagreement with something that one of them has said, she renews her calls for order.

While this is taking place, Milon has started towards the podium to join Paula and Dr. Joy. Order is restored and the chair recognizes Dulfa, the representative from Region sixteen. She is a younger female; dumpy in her dress and style. She is dressed in a neon, lime green jumpsuit with a neon-orange vest. Her hair is a purposeful total disaster and tinted a bright blue. This female has been standing in the aisle and shouting and waving her arms in the air. She shouts now even though the general commotion has abated.

"I object! I object to this *unlawful* intrusion! I most *vehemently* object! To this, to this *obstruction* of due process!"

She's now yelling full voice. "I object to this vulgar demonstration. This unprecedented outrage. In the entire history of our great Femeron..."

"Relax, Dulfa," Paula leans over to speak into the microphone and interrupts her from the podium. "They aren't going to rape *you*!"

There is laughter in the hall and several other females shout out other smart put downs. Dulfa is stroke dumb.

Paula directs herself toward the chair. "I request re-recognition in order that we might complete our presentation."

Before the chair can respond, Dulfa shouts out in a very authoritarian voice, "I must object to this request." Dulfa bangs on her console to get the attention of the chair. "Might I remind the presiding officers that this *entire* proceeding is out of order. The rules of the Summit of Assemblies specifically do not allow such...such displays and demonstrations."

As Dulfa is speaking one of her aides has found a section of the Summit Parliamentary Rules and Procedures. She hustles this hologram page over to Dulfa's console and Dulfa, without missing a beat, begins to read it out loud.

"Article Nine, Section A states that 'any continual disturbance which keeps the Summit Assembly from being capable of completing their discussions; will be ruled by the majority vote of the presiding officials to be out of order. If such ruling is made, then the individuals identified by the chairperson, shall be requested to either cease such disturbance or to leave the summit assembly hall forthwith.'"

"Thank you for bringing that to our attention," The chair lady responds sarcastically. "The chair is well aware of this code section, Dulfa but as far as I can see, there is no disturbance at the moment except yours and therefore no need to invoke this rule."

The assembly hall has gotten quiet but Dulfa does not relent in her attempt to silence Dr. Joy's presentation.

"I maintain that this *entire* discussion has been a disturbance! And it continues to disrupt our purpose here."

"That purpose," Paula interrupts, "is to decide a course of action. Our presentation is in that direction and perfectly within the rules."

"Your presentation is *ridiculous!*" Dulfa is beside herself. "You've been misguided by this...this *outcast* scientist. Your logic...her logic ignores the facts, the historical facts!"

"Nonsense," Paula smirks and waves the back of her hand at Dulfa. "My belief in Dr. Joy's solution is based on the fact that it will work! And my opinion is that it will work safely if the proper controls are adhered to."

"Ridiculous!" Dulfa shouts. "I request that the presiding officers vote to end this continual disturbance."

The chairperson confers with the other ten Femeron officials at the center console. While they are talking, Paula, Dr. Joy and Milon huddle up at the podium.

"This isn't looking good," Paula says. "If it goes to a vote of the central committee I fear they'll side with Dulfa."

"Before Milon can even speak to them?" Dr. Joy asks.

"Yes, I'm afraid so."

"I thought this was a democratic republic?" Milon says.

"Yes, it is," Paula says. "Yes, it certainly is!"

She steps up the podium and her amplified voice is carried over the assembly hall. "If there is to be vote on whether a duly elected official may present a proposal to the assembly, then I request that the vote be made by the entire assembly."

"Article One, Section A," Paula adds the proper code section for the assembly to consider. "One person, one vote."

The assembly is a buzz now with agreement to Paula's point. Another Femeron representative is given the floor and she shouts out from the front of her console. "I request that the chair overrules Dulfa's objections and allows the speaker to continue uninterrupted by anymore of *her* disturbances!"

By the positive murmurings resounding throughout the assembly the summit hall appears to concur with this motion. The chairperson, seeing that this is the obvious majority opinion, says; "I so rule." After a short discussion with her panel, she adds, "Paula, you have the floor."

"Thank you," Paula does a half bow to the chairperson. "I would like to introduce you all to a male that was bred, born and raised right here in Femeron." She points to Milon with a wave of her entire arm and hand. "His name is, Milon. Milon if you would, please."

Milon takes a slow, deep breath and walks to the front of the podium and looks out across the large hall.

"G'day, Boys and Girls," Milon says and the auditorium is filled with thunderous boos and spontaneous laughter.

Dr. Joy runs the palm of her right hand across her forehead and over her hair.

"My debate instructor quoting Winston Churchill, always advised us that a speech should be like a lady's skirt. Long enough to cover the subject but short enough to keep our attention."

Again, loud boos but a greater sprinkling of laughter. "I will follow her advice as I attempt to convince you that I am normal, like you. You are normal, right?" He laughs at his own joke and the audience shout out loud 'yes' and 'no' responses.

"Good, so we have that much going for us."

He pauses, looks around at the faces below him. "I find myself at the podium of the Femeron's Summit Council addressing the most powerful people on the planet. The rulers of our society, yes, it is *our* society, even though you have defined my place in it and have all but removed me from its benefits, still, I am a part of it. As are all of the males that have been imprisoned, not because of individual actions, but because we as an entire sex have been defined to be inferior. Deficient. Isn't that how you describe us?"

He leans forward and says gently, "Somehow I am to convince you, through verbal communication, words, and words alone that I am a human being. A complete human being, no more or less than yourselves. How do I do that? How do I show the truth in such a way that it can be seen by everyone?"

Milon pauses again for a longer moment. His speech is not rehearsed and he is thinking of what words to use. He continues in a more forceful manner. "I claim to be your equal. I did not say superior. I did not say almost equal. I said I am your equal. I am an individual. I have strengths and weaknesses. I seek happiness and self-fulfillment. I search for inner peace. I see life as a miracle and I only wish to know more about its endless dimensions. I strive to obtain a higher consciousness so

I may better understand my life and the world around me." He pauses, looks into the faces before him and continues. "I ask you to please allow me the freedom to seek these things in my lifetime." He stops and shakes his head, looks around the large room at the many faces now attentive to his words. Still shaking his head, he says, "I wonder, can you know me from just these few words? Can you judge me based upon a few minutes talk? I ask you to please weigh the vibrations of my being as much as you consider my words." He pauses, laughs and says, much more intense now.

"The individual. What is his or hers' worth? Is that worth dictated by the people around us or is it received from within ourselves? I believe that if you nurture a child; nurture them with love for themselves. If you nurture their self-esteem, then that child, those children, will love life and the good people in it."

Milon is speaking now as if he were talking personally to each person in the audience. As if to a friend. He is open and relaxed.

"Well, have I convinced you? I think I have. I have faith in your humanness, in our common humanness. But I don't think that is all that is in question here. I think it comes down to whether or not you'll accept a male as a Femeron leader. Is that not the ultimate end if you do choose to free us? Are you not then voting on that possibility? I think you are and I think that many of you fear that possibility. After all, if you do set us free, if you allow us to enter into Femeron society as equals, we will exercise our rights and among those rights are the rights to free thoughts and speech. You must expect that someday a male will speak his mind. He may even attract supporters to his ideas. Can you accept the fact that such an individual could be elected to sit as a leader among you? Do you fear that possibility? If you do, I am here to tell you, your fears are not valid. They are not valid because your citizens are not naïve children. They have their own minds and must be respected. Whether you have a valid fear of placing males back into positions of power or not, the point is, are you willing to put the Femeron society, the great Femeron culture, through this ultimate test of freedom?"

He pauses, then says, "When you vote, I ask only that you weigh this consciously. If your vote be nay, then let it be nay because it is your intellect and not a nay cast from the depths of fear."

Milon smiles, then finishes by saying, "I bid you peace."

Paula steps forward and shouts over the applause. "I request that a vote be taken on the proposal now before this summit meeting."

"Not so fast," Dulfa jumps out of her seat and speaks up. "One male seems a pretty picture of reasonableness. We cannot, should not cast ballots based upon one alone. I want to choose another male, from among those here."

"Go ahead, choose one," Dr. Joy challenges her.

"Okay, there. That vagrant looking one." Dulfa points to Paul as he leans against the wall nearest her console.

He winks at her and walks to the speaker's podium. As he walks up the carpeted steps, Dr. Joy and Paula greet him.

"No, Girlie, comments, please," Dr. Joy says into his ear as they touch cheeks. Paul, laughs. He is taller than them and has to lean over to touch cheeks with Paula.

He then steps to the podium. He smiles. His blond hair and blue eyes sparkle with charisma. His dimple cheeks and cleft chin exude his charm.

"What this is all about," he begins in a strong but calm voice, "is how we can manage to deal with one another and especially with people with whom we don't agree. How are we to deal with people who we in fact hate? Can we find a way to resolve our issues without resorting to acts of violence or deceit?" Paul lets the question hang in the air.

"Well, sure. Let's just teach people not to hate. A simple answer, yes and one that does not work. Turns out that hate is built into our psyche. Turns out that it is one of our most basic emotions. It is a natural human emotion for people to hate each other and history is replete with examples. It is possible, in fact probable, that there has *never* been a time when people have not hated. For many thousands of years hatred has been a key ingredient in relations between peoples and especially between peoples of different cultures, religions and ethnicity. Isn't it about time that we as a society make an effort to deal with this the most destructive of human emotions?"

He pauses, again to let the question hang in the air.

"But I warn you, there should be no expectation that it can be erased from the human genome. I fear it is too basic a human trait to try to eradicate it from the human heart. No, what we must do, what we must spend time and money and energy on, is to work on educating people in the least destructive ways to deal with one's *own* hatred." Paul points to the females. "Come on be honest! We've all hated someone or some group of people. Not our finest moment, but it is a natural emotion. One we usually respond to by trying to damage the object of our hate."

He pauses again to gather his thoughts,

"People try to damage those that are the objects of their hatred. I'm no scientist but what I have seen is that despite our intentions to hurt the target of our hate, we see the recipient time and again, respond in the *exact* opposite way then what we wanted. That's right, people react opposite to your intentions. If I curse him, he curses me back. If I attack her ways or her traditions that offend me, she will proudly celebrate those very traditions and will *attack* my way of living! If we threaten them with violence, it is certain that we, the haters, will reap violence as our reward."

Paul looks around and shakes his head. "So, you see, we are not going to stop people from hating, but what we must try to do, is to get them to not *act* out with hatred. I think the only way to do that is to make them see that it is in *their* self-interest not to do so. We have to educate people throughout the world and in many different cultures. Educate the followers of different religions that it is in their self- interest not to resort to violence or deceit. Not because it isn't nice, or fair or is evil and hurts the other person, after all that is precisely what they want to do. Hurt the other fellow. If we want to stop the destructive results of hatred, we must develop a system of education which teaches that it is in their own self-interest not to strike out in hatred.

We must show people that reacting with violence and deceit will *always, always* bring bad results to them. Not only to them but to their families, to their friends and yes, to their communities."

Paul finishes in a determined, strong voice. "This needs further, detailed research. We need to put our best people on it. We need to make it of the highest priority.

"I'm Paul and that's how I see it. Thank you for allowing me to address you today."

Paul backs away from the podium and stands with his hands at his sides. He smiles at the spattering of applause, led by Dr. Joy, Paula, Milon and their staffs. The applause grows and finally Paul acknowledges it with a short bow and wave of his hand.

Paula steps forward to the front of the podium. She has to shout even with the aid of the public address system, as the assembly is still quite uproarious after the two male speeches. "I request a vote be taken on the proposal now before this Summit Council."

Over the din of noise, Paula's motion is seconded by many other Femeron representatives who shout their approval from the floor of the great hall. The chairperson has been repeatedly calling for order and when a semblance is restored, she announces; "There has been placed before us an alternative proposal to the solutions offered by the Cloning Research and Advisory Committee. We have all seen and heard the arguments for and against and we will now put this matter to a vote. I am requesting that the duly elected Femeron representatives cast their vote for their region over the tele-computer. Each representative please identify now."

The Femeron representatives each places their thumbs over their console's keypad which allows the main computer to identify and verify each of them. As this is being done, the large screen on the wall behind the officials shows a green light for each region. As the

94 regions each turn on, the assembly is ready to enter their votes and the computer is ready to tally them. The message across the screen and across each individual console screen reads:

OFFICIAL VOTE: ACCEPT YES NO

As each representative enters their vote a red light goes on next to that region's green light. When each green light has a red light next to it, the chair lady announces that the voting has ended.

"The voting has ended," she says again. "Will the Secretary Officer please display the results?"

One of the women at the presiding table nods her head and inputs instructions onto her keypad. On the video screens, large and small throughout the assembly hall the results come up in tall, white lights.

YES 73 NO 21

As soon as these number flash across the screen, the summit hall bursts into a spontaneous reaction. Excitement fills the room as members from all of the supporting delegations applaud and discuss among themselves the meaning of their success. Those that opposed the proposal, pull their hair in anger and frustration and immediately begin their plans to nullify the election in any way possible. Dulfa conferring with Meangala hints that there is an "Insurance Plan" in place that will nullify the outrageous results of this vote.

# Chapter Nine
## Back Story: Paul Sr.

Year: 2045

Location: City on the West Coast of the former United States of America

It wasn't until evening when Paul Sr. rolled into what the locals called Ciudad de An-hey- lees. He left the bus station and walked towards the Galapagos Room, a throwback bar in Santa Monica where he was to meet his friend, Victor. He had to stay alert as he walked along the garbage strewn sidewalk as there were bands of roving young people lying in ambush, ready and willing to attack anyone, strip them bare and kill them if need be to get what they wanted.

Orange flames from trash barrels lit the darkened street. Black smoke rose up slow and dirty from them. Trash, loose papers, sewage and human waste ran in the gutters. Each street had hovels made from boxes and plastic tents along the sidewalk. There were hundreds of homeless living in these tent neighborhoods and hundreds more that had taken over the office buildings and apartment houses along the street. These families had converted them into small, shared apartments. There was no electricity so candles burned in windows. Water was carried in from hoses that still ran water or from opened fire hydrants although that was at last resort because they tended to flood the streets and the homeless camped outside didn't like their stuff to get wet.

Victor was standing outside the bar's green door under a darkened electric sign. He was tall and skinny with dark hair and six-day beard. He had been born and raised in the Bronx and it showed in his accent and urban style.

"Hey, Victor. How's it going?" Paul Sr. pumped fists with him.

"Yeah, it's going all right," Victor responded, checking and keeping an eye on a group of kids across the street who were watching him and Paul too closely.

"C'mon in, we'll get a drink." He motioned to the door and held it open for Paul.

It was dark inside. Music played but not so loud that they couldn't hear themselves. A few men were shooting eight ball at an old fashion, slate pool table. Paul looked around. The bar was only half full. The smell of pizza and pee was pretty strong as he and Victor took their seats. Victor ordered two beers and the barkeep slid them down to them. Paul took a long swig and looked around the room again.

"A throwback bar copying the style from the nineteen eighties," Victor said. "It used to be a pretty nice place until the neighborhood got crushed with migrants and homeless."

"Is the whole city this way?" Paul asked.

"Yeah, well everywhere except the wealthy neighborhoods."

"And there?"

"They each have to have armed guards 24/7."

"And if they don't?"

"Then they come home to find that they have been mob rushed; everything taken, everything of value gone or destroyed. The rushers like to destroy what they can't carry."

"Mob rush?"

"A group of people rush into a store or a residence and just overwhelm the place. They take whatever they want, do whatever they want and the store owners or home owners just have to watch."

"Can't they fight back?"

"What are you going to do? Fight 40 or 50 people? Or shoot and kill 40 or 50? Then you go to prison for murder or for owning a firearm which hasn't been legal in twenty years."

"What happens to the owners after their stuff is robbed?" Paul asked.

"Mostly, when they've been had like that, people just leave and get the hell out." Victor took a sip of his beer. "Then their place fills up with three, four, five families and they camp there without electricity or water."

"No plumbing?"

"No, of course not."

"Rough," Paul said.

"Yeah, rough but better than from where they've come from."

"Where they've come from? Okay, what's it like now in Bombay then? New Delhi? Shanghai?"

"Much worse," Victor shrugged.

"Hard to imagine, much worse."

"Much worse, trust me."

"I do. But where is this going? Can you imagine fifty years from now, a hundred?" Paul asked.

"I've heard it said that the earth will cleanse itself," Victor said. "Some people say there will be diseases without cures, violent deaths, wars."

"It will have to be pretty drastic," Paul said. "I mean for a disease or war to kill off a billion people."

"That might not even be enough," Victor said. "I read somewhere that we've already passed the tipping point. There is nothing that can be done now to reverse the population explosion. And the consequences."

"Maybe an asteroid strike?" Paul smiles. Victor doesn't. "I meant is as a joke."

"Yeah, right. We're down to rooting for an asteroid to strike the earth," Victor says, not amused.

The light from the neon sign over the bar changed colors and Paul noticed that Victor's hair morphed from silver to green to pink as they spoke. He thought it must be the beer going to his head.

"And for the wealthy families?" Paul asks.

"They've done the best they can for themselves, of course," Victor says.

Paul nods. "They always do."

"Yes, and why not? Wouldn't you do the best you could for your children? For your family?"

"Of course."

"Most of the wealthy families have moved away," Victor went on. "They've gone to the Midwest or down south or even up into Canada."

"That's too cold for me," Paul says.

"Yeah, me too."

"But at least they got away from this... this shit hole," Paul says.

"Well they may have been able to isolate themselves from the violent poverty," Victor says, "but their world is still reduced. They can't travel. It's too dangerous to go anywhere now. If you have something, anything, there are hordes of people wanting to take it from you. And they are ready and able. They will break any window, smash any wall and overwhelm any hired guard to get to you and the things they want. The wealthy families' quality of life is reduced. The loss of habitat, the continued loss of animal species. Everything, is being devoured by the unstoppable human population explosion."

Paul nods his understanding.

"The governments worked so hard and spent so much on ridding the world of disease," Victor continues. "And all the social programs they paid for. Their desire to help the poor only increased the population. Yet the people of those over-populated countries, India, China, Africa, they give no thought to the resources needed to maintain their children. And all of them wanting more. More food, more technology, more things. And it's not their fault either; it's basic human nature to want to eat and have shelter and enjoy the many benefits of modern life."

"So, trying to make things better, led to making things worse?" Paul asked. He shook his head in disbelief to the idea that the people who meant well, had in fact helped increase the run-away population problem.

"They made things much worse." Victor finished his beer and ordered two more. When they came, he paid and continued to reflect on the problem as he saw it.

"The wealthy families now are competing to survive as a dynasty. They're using genetic enhancing technology to insure the continuation of their genes. They want their own flesh and blood established before the 'weeding out' takes place."

"We use to read how the world needed and thrived on diversity," Paul said, "but I don't see it thriving now or into the future."

"No," Victor agreed, "it's going to be a mess going forward. It isn't going to thrive either; not with twice the population to feed and clothe and house."

"No, not thrive," Paul agreed.

"No, not thrive. Sure-as-shit-not-thrive," Victor said with emotion. "It's gonna be a mess and you know what I think?" Victor waited for Paul's response.

"What's that, Victor?"

"Women are going to rule the planet."

"They already do," Paul it said as a joke.

"No, I don't mean as ball busters. I mean rule it as in Washington and Moscow and Bejing."

"Maybe their due a chance at it," Paul said.

"Oh, they're going to get the chance all right. The problem is they hate men because they never will understand us."

"What do you mean?" Paul asked.

"They can relate to kids and animals and the underdog but to men? Never."

"Never?"

"No. They will never understand how sex rules over us. They can't relate to that. How could they? They've never had a throbbing hard-on bouncing on their bellies in the middle of the night."

"No, I guess not," Paul said.

Victor laughed then said, "I'm serious. Men are horny and women won't ever forgive them for that. They won't forgive the human race for developing the way it has, with men dominating life and them weak sisters."

"Forgive us? Probably not," Paul said. "But they need us. Can't make babies without us."

"Actually, they're pretty close to doing just that," Victor answered.

"How do they do that?" Paul asked.

"They are close, very close to perfecting cloning," Victor said. "When they have that, they won't need us except maybe the horny ones."

Paul laughed.

"Haven't you seen the commercials where they show women beating men at shooting pool, then at arm wrestling?" Victor asked. "All their bullshit power fantasies in Wonder Woman and Super Girl? But they're going to make up for it. You wait and see. They are going to use their numbers to put themselves into power and when they do, watch out. They know how to lie and cheat and frame everything in such a way, that they can rationalize all of their actions."

Paul and Victor drank and ate at the bar until the days' long journey caught up with Paul and he and Victor got a ride to the motel where Paul had made reservations to stay. Victor headed home and Paul readied for bed but once settled in, his mind held onto the vision of the streets with open sewers and abandoned children. It was sometime after 4am when he finally dozed off only to be woken by a loud crash as the front door was being broken into. He jumped up, couldn't find his pants, searched frantically for his underwear and just managed to pull them up when storm troopers broke through the door and ran into the room.

"Hands up! Hands Up!" They shouted in a strange accent. A combination Russian/Nigerian slant of English.

They wore short shorts and tank tops and that made Paul laugh at the sight of them but then four of the officers aimed chrome bars at his head. He didn't find them funny at all after that.

"Okay, okay," he said as he raised his hands in the air.

The officers were serious and certainly intent on arresting him, yet they seemed quite feminine in their movements and speech. Were they males? But they wore heavy eye makeup and lipstick. They had strange tattoos on their necks and their hair was cut in sharp angles and dyed jet black with chartreuse highlights.

"Who are you?" Paul asked while they searched his belongings.

"Never mind that," one of them answered. He shoved Paul towards the door. Paul was surprised because the officer's push was weak and hardly moved him.

"I need my clothes," Paul said as he tried to turn around to collect his pants.

"Just move it. Now!" the same little one struck him in the stomach with the chrome bar and it hurt.

In his underwear, Paul walked out through the door hanging from its broken hinges, to a shiny, aluminum vehicle waiting at the curb.

"Strange," Paul thought, "I don't see any wheels."

They all five got into the vehicle and it rose into the air a foot or two and traveled slowly down the street. Paul looked out and saw sewage in the gutter and more bands of youths running up the sidewalk, away from the Police cruiser. Around the corner, a building was on fire.

"Where is this?" Paul asked. "What's happened?"

"What's happened where?" the officer next to him in the back seat asked. Paul could still not tell their sex.

"Here. This is Los Angeles, right?"

"Ciudad de Angeles, si. Doesn't it look like it?"

"It looks like Hell on earth." Paul said and the officer stared at him annoyed.

Outside, as they passed the burning building, the poor inhabitants stood in the street clutching their few possessions. Other groups of people gathered to watch.

"Where is the Fire Department?" Paul shouted, not understanding the policemen's' nonchalance.

"The Flame Control people don't serve this district," the officer in the passenger seat said over his shoulder.

"They don't serve...why not?" Paul asked.

"Look around A-Hole. Do these people look like taxpayers to you?" the same officer answered.

"No tax, no service," the officer in the back said with a smile.

"Cash economy means no taxes being paid," the officer driving added and they all laughed.

"You see, they cheat the system," the driver said, "but then they expect services for free. It doesn't work that way no more."

"They really did make it worse for themselves," the front officer says and Paul had to agree.

Paul saw hundreds of homeless people roaming the dark streets. Rows of plastic tents and dirty blankets lined the sidewalks and gutters. After a half hour ride, the squad car pulled into an underground parking lot beneath a government complex in downtown Angel City. Paul was taken upstairs by two of the officers where he was booked then brought to a holding cell.

"I really need to get some clothes on, don't you think?" he asked the guard who locked him up into a small cell with a glass door.

"Oh, I don't know," the guard said with a smile. "You've certainly caught the eye of some of our other quests."

"Exactly what I mean and I'm cold."

"All right, don't go all bitchy on me," the guard laughed. "I'll see what I can find for you."

That evening along with his meal, another guard brought a stack of orange prison garb, socks and a paper-thin blanket. Paul could get only a partial night's sleep and, in the morning, after a cup of cold soup for breakfast, he was visited by a female in civilian dress.

"Paul Windsor?" she asked him through his cell door.

"Yes," Paul said as he got up and walked over to her.

"Bring him to the interrogation room, please," she commanded the officer with her.

The officer, dressed in short shorts and wearing make-up, led them down the hall to another room with glass walls. Paul sat across from the female and watched her closely as she took out a hologram file from her watch, expanded it and showed it to him.

"I'm Susan Swift from the United States Genetics Laboratory Research Division."

"And?" Paul said, not understanding why she was there to see him.

"And, I'm here because your genetic chromosome configuration has been selected by our planning program's computer for inclusion into our cloning program."

"Try saying that three times fast," Paul laughed.

"What part did you not understand?" she asked without smiling.

"Oh, I understood all the words, but what is it that you want of me?"

"It's your lucky day, actually," she said with a phony smile.

"Yeah, feels that way to me too. But I still don't even know why I've been arrested and locked up?"

"That was on our orders for the locals to find and hold you until I could get here."

"I see. Well I'm not very happy about you doing that. Why didn't you just contact me directly?"

"I'm not really sure how that was all arranged to be honest with you. Still, I think you'll find that it was all worthwhile."

"Being hauled away in my briefs? It better be good." "It's beyond good, Mister Windsor. To be included into the cloning program means a life of leisure and...well, luxury."

"Leisure and Luxury, huh?"

"I think you will find the program most rewarding," she said, taking back the hologram image from him.

"And if I don't opt for leisure and luxury?" he asked. "How disappointed will your people be?"

"Very, I'm afraid. You see we don't calculate refusals into our statistics. Your genes have been selected by the main government computer and so your genes will be included in the pool."

"I see." Paul studied her for several moments. She was young with short hair dyed in three colors. Her complexion was very clean, soft and smooth. He liked her brown eyes and thin lips. At least they sent a temptress, he thought to himself.

"I am fully authorized to have you released into my custody for the return trip back into Femeron."

"And once I'm there?"

"Once you're there, you will be given living quarters and provided with all the services and needs you require to live a happy life."

"My own apartment? Or shared dwelling?"

"Your own, one-bedroom apartment."

"Two bedrooms. I'll need at least two."

"Two? Why two?" she asked with real surprise.

"I want to use one for my office and studio."

"I see. Okay, yes, I can have you placed into one of the larger units if that's what it takes to have your full cooperation."

Paul stopped to consider.

"Do you golf, Mister Windsor?" she asked.

"Golf? I've played yes. Why?"

"Because the residence sits on a very nice golf facility. You would be provided with a full membership."

"I see," Paul nodded.

"Yes, and there are other amenities. Like swimming pools, restaurants, and social activities."

Paul didn't react, trying to decide.

"And if I say no?" he finally asked her.

"No? Huh...Well if you say no, Mister Windsor, I will leave here and you will be prosecuted for whatever crimes they find convenient to hang on you."

"So, it's a toss-up then." Paul half smiled at her.

"A toss up? Not how I see it."

"That was sarcasm, girl," Paul said.

"Sarcasm? I see. And it was probably sarcasm that got you to this point. If I were you, I'd drop the sarcasm,

Mister Windsor. And I would definitely drop the 'girl' appellations. That's just asking for trouble."

"A bit touchy, are we?"

"Touchy?"

"Never mind. So, what do I have to do in return for this life of the rich and famous?"

"Your semen will be collected on an assigned schedule."

"Collected?"

"Yes, in a laboratory."

"By whom?"

"By laboratory workers, of course."

"But without intercourse?"

"I'm afraid not. That is not part of the prescribed procedures."

"Well I suppose it beats living in an orange jumpsuits."

"By far, Mister Windsor. By far."

\*\*\*

In the weeks that followed, Paul was transferred east of the Rocky Mountains, through the extreme border security into Femeron. He was moved into a two-bedroom apartment, the corner unit of an upscale apartment complex on the grounds of a large golf course and country club. That was in the year 2045. The genes that he provided to the cloning project were the foundation for all of the Paul's to follow, including Paul, Milon's friend and speaker at the Femeron Grand Council.

Lightning Source UK Ltd.
Milton Keynes UK
UKHW040933201020
371904UK00001B/153